The Kennedy Boys

The Irish Getaway
A Standalone Short Novel

SIOBHAN DAVIS
www.siobhandavis.com

Copyright © Siobhan Davis 2017. Siobhan Davis asserts the moral right to be identified as the author of this work. All rights reserved under International and Pan-American Copyright Conventions.

This is a work of fiction. Names, characters, places, incidents and dialogues are products of the author's imagination or are used fictitiously. Any resemblance to actual people, living or dead, or events is entirely coincidental.

This book is sold subject to the condition that it shall not, by way of trade or otherwise be lent, resold, hired out or otherwise circulated without the prior written consent of the author. No part of this publication may be reproduced, transmitted, decompiled, or stored in or introduced into any information storage and retrieval system, in any form or by any means, whether electronic or mechanical, including photocopying, without the author's written permission.

Printed by Createspace, An Amazon.com Company
Paperback edition © September 2018

ISBN-13: 978-1725970564
ISBN-10: 1725970562

Editor: Kelly Hartigan (XterraWeb) editing.xterraweb.com
Cover design by Robin Harper https://wickedbydesigncovers.wixsite.com
The Irish Getaway Image © depositphotos.com
Inseparable Image © istockphoto.com
Loving Kalvin and Saving Brad Photos by Sara Eirew Photographer
Formatting by The Deliberate Page www.deliberatepage.com

Note From The Author

You should only read this novel if you have already read *Finding Kyler*, *Losing Kyler*, and *Keeping Kyler*. If you haven't read these books yet, this short novel will spoil the story for you.

Dedication

For my lovely sister-in-law, Sinead Davis. Thanks for suggesting I write this! I'm hugely grateful for your constant support and encouragement.

Chapter One

Faye

"Well? What do you think? Will I do?" I spin around on my strappy stilettos, facing Ky as I show off the uber-short cream and gold mini-dress that hugs my body like a second skin. For the second year in a row, Ireland is experiencing an unforeseen Indian summer that is playing havoc with my thick hair, so I've pinned it up into a messy-on-purpose bun with longish strands curled and framing my face. My makeup is pristine, my eyes smoky and rimmed in lashings of thick black liner thanks to my friend Rachel. She's the makeup magician, the style queen, the reason I'm currently feeling like a million dollars.

Between Rach and Alex, I've had no choice but to embrace my inner femininity, surprising myself in the process because I don't detest getting dolled up like I used to. In fact, since Ky and I became a couple, I've been dressing up more. Not because I want to look good for him—although, *naturally* I do—but mainly because I feel like I've finally grown into my body, embraced my sexuality, and I'm confident in my own skin.

Strong, warm hands grip my waist as Ky tugs me toward him, his eyes darkening with lust. "You look hot, sexy as all hell." He leans in to kiss me, but I wiggle out of his embrace.

"Nuh-uh." I shake my head, sending him a stern look. "Our guests will be arriving any minute now, and I know what'll happen if I let you kiss me." We can scarcely keep our hands off one another, and it's borderline worrisome. To crave someone as much as I crave him doesn't seem normal. Or not the normal I'm used to.

"Babe." His eyes gleam with wicked intent. "Let's cancel the party and start our own private one. I want you all to myself." His tongue darts out, licking his full lips, and it's like an injection of liquid lust straight through my veins.

I curse under my breath. "Ky. You've had me all to yourself these last two weeks." It's the truth. Apart from hanging with my besties a few times, we've spent every single second of every minute of every day of our vacation together. And it's truly been like a piece of heaven on Earth. We can't get enough of one another, and I love it. But we've only one week until the rest of the family lands on Irish soil, and I want to make the most of it.

Starting with this party.

I've missed my extended group of friends, and it'll be good to catch up with old school buddies. Besides, I promised myself before I returned home that I would make new memories in this house so that I'm not accosted with overwhelming grief and sadness every time I step over the threshold.

Ky has been helping with that. A blush creeps up my neck and across my cheeks as I remember all the ways he's been *helping* me. I quietly laugh to myself.

This party will work wonders too. This house needs to be filled with laughter and music and the sounds of many voices.

Ky smirks, recognizing where my mind has gone. He takes a step toward me, and I take a step back. "I have been monopolizing you, haven't I?" He cocks his head to the side as he continues advancing like a predator with sole focus. I back up some more until my spine meets the solid wall behind me. Pressing his body against mine, he places his hands on either side of my head and leans into my face. His warm, intoxicating breath blows over my skin, and a familiar ache starts building inside me. It's ridiculous how much I'm attracted to him and how powerless I am to resist. "I've had you on the stairs, in the shower, on the kitchen counter, on the couch, against the wall outside, in your—"

"Oh my God! Enough!" I shriek, attempting to compose myself. One of us needs to stay focused. A difficult task when my legs have turned to jelly and my body is already trembling with need. "Is there a point to this?"

Quick as a flash, his hand juts out, and he swats the entire contents lining the top of my dressing table onto the floor. My jaw slackens as he grips my hips, lifting me fluidly onto the wooden tabletop. He inches the hem of my dress up, and my legs automatically open for him, like the Red Sea parting for Moses. There's no point even attempting to fight it.

He presses a slew of drugging kisses along my jawline as he loosens the button on his jeans. "I haven't had you here, and we have enough time." A devilish expression is etched on his face. "Unless you're not interested." His hand stalls on his jeans as he straightens up, challenging me with his eyes.

As if.

I growl, fisting a hand in his shirt and pulling him toward me. "Asshole."

He chuckles. "You can't resist me any more than I can resist you."

My hand replaces his as I yank his jeans and boxers down in one swift movement. "What have you done to me?" I ask, my voice coming out low and seductive. Taking him in my hand, I fondle him in firm, confident strokes, licking my lips in anticipation.

A strangled sound emits from his throat as he pushes my flimsy, lacy thong to one side, thrusting two fingers inside me. I gasp, already soaking wet for him, and my strokes become quicker. "The same thing you've done to me," he confirms before crashing his mouth atop mine. His kiss consumes me, and, even though we've kissed, like, a million times, each time he kisses me, it feels like the first time. Tingling sensations ignite my entire body, and I arch toward him, needy and hungry. No measure of time with Ky will be long enough to satisfy the unerring craving I have for him. My body comes alive at his touch, and I hope it never stops.

I guide him toward me, stretching my legs out wider as he enters me in one fast thrust. Now that we're exclusive, and I'm on the pill, we don't bother with condoms anymore. We discussed it at length, making the decision together. We're in this forever, and I can't see any reason not to take this next step. We trust each other, and there is no greater feeling than the love of my life buried deep inside me with nothing separating us.

I close my eyes, taking a moment to truly feel him. And it's not just the physical connection. When we're together like this, it's as if our souls are entwined. And even though we're as close as two people can get, I still crave more. I never knew it could be like this. That I could feel so much love in my heart for a boy. That I could feel so complete. He is everything to me. Everything I didn't realize I wanted or needed until he was in my life. Embedded so deep into every facet of my existence that sometimes I almost forget where I start and he ends.

But I wouldn't have it any other way.

I love him as deeply as he loves me, and I know, without a shadow of a doubt, that he's my forever.

I whimper into his mouth as he starts moving, my legs wrapping around his waist like an octopus. His tongue darts out, seeking entry, and I open my lips, allowing him to explore me as I explore him. The dressing table rattles and wobbles underneath me, but I'm barely conscious of the noise as Ky pounds into me, harder and faster, and I'm rapidly spinning out of control. I dig my nails into his shoulder and suck on his lower lip, dragging it between my teeth.

"I fucking love you," he cries, thrusting deeper. "You undo me, Faye."

"I forever you" is all I can manage to get out in between moans. Our kissing grows more frantic, and I plunder his mouth as desire ignites the fire inside me. The crescendo gaining momentum inside me is reaching epic proportions, and I'm close to the edge. The dressing table screeches as the back of it slaps against the wall, but Ky doesn't stop, thrusting over and over until I scream, crying out his name as waves of pure bliss rock my body. He grunts and roars my name as his own release arrives, and we cling to each other, bodies heaving, heart rates elevated, panting and gasping for air. "Ho. Lee. Shit. Ky." I lower my quivering legs to the floor and he leans in, placing a feather-soft kiss on my lips, at complete odds with the way he just devoured my body.

"It gets me every time, baby." He drags a hand through his silky dark hair, attempting to tame it. "I only have to look at you and I get hard. I'll never get enough, Faye. Never."

I don't need convincing. We've been going at it like rabbits since we arrived here, and my attraction to him is every bit as potent as his is to me. I've never felt this way about anyone before. No one has ever rocked my world like Ky has. Not a day goes by where I don't thank my lucky stars for bringing him to me. I snake my arms around his neck. "I hope not because I'm never letting you go."

He presses a kiss to the top of my head. "That's music to my ears, babe." I rest my head on his shoulder, and his arms envelop me in a hug. We stay like that for a couple of minutes, and a wave of contentment washes over me. Everything has always felt right with the world once Ky is by my side.

"I'll get a towel. Stay here," he says after a bit, kissing my forehead as he eases out of our embrace. I don't move while he leaves my bedroom to retrieve a washcloth from the bathroom. When he returns, he cleans me up, helping me fix my underwear and my dress.

I survey the wreckage on the floor and the new skid marks on the wall where the dresser scraped against the paint with a knowing smile. We're definitely making new memories. Not sure my parents would wholeheartedly approve, but I like to think they'd be happy I'm in a good place in my life. That I have the love and support of a good guy.

Ky is helping me put everything back on the dresser when the doorbell chimes. "Can you get that while I fix my hair and makeup?"

He frowns at me. "You look perfect."

I roll my eyes. *Men.* Rachel would take one look at the state of me and know what just happened, freaking over the mess I've made of her hair and makeup job. I give him a gentle shove toward the door. "Go. I'll be two minutes. Entertain the masses until then."

When I emerge a few minutes later, I find my man in the center of the living room surrounded by a bunch of my school friends. Every girl is staring up at him with glazed eyes. I quietly snicker as I approach them, sliding my arm around his waist. "Hey, thanks so much for coming."

Reluctantly, they drag their gaze away from the hot Kennedy boy by my side, taking turns to hug me. More and more guests arrive, and I'm separated from Ky as I rush to get everyone settled with drinks. Soon the small living room is crammed with bodies. Jill—my other bestie—sets up the sound system with her boyfriend, Sam, in the corner of the room, and the crowd hollers as kickass rhythmic beats pump out.

Rach is on door duty, and soon the whole house is packed to capacity with bodies lining the passageway, filling the living room and kitchen. Everyone wants to hear about my life in America, and I haven't had a second to even catch my breath. Every so often, I steal a glimpse at

Ky, and he seems to be enjoying himself. I don't miss the numerous admiring glances my ex-schoolmates throw his way, but I don't care. I'm secure in his love. They can ogle him all they want, but, at the end of the day, he's mine and I'm his, and nothing or no one will ever come between us again.

"It's like a sauna in here," Rach complains, arriving in the kitchen, fanning her face with her hand.

"I know, but I've opened all the windows, and there isn't anything else I can do. We are not equipped for this kind of climate."

"We should've had the party at my house." She pours a large gin and tonic into a glass, dumping some ice and basil leaves on top. "We've got state-of-the-art air conditioning." There's an edge to her tone that I can't decipher. Rach's parents won the lottery about ten months ago, and her life has transformed. They moved out of their small terraced three-bed house into a sprawling mansion on the outskirts of town. My eyes had been out on stalks when she invited us over for lunch the first week we were here. Sporting ten en suite bedrooms, four large reception rooms, a kitchen I'd happily trade a limb for, an indoor swimming pool, sauna, gym, cinema, and outdoor tennis courts, it gives the Kennedy house in Wellesley a run for its money.

"Probably, but I kinda wanted to have it here anyway."

Her look softens as she takes a sip of her drink. "I understand. How have things been?"

"Good." I try to fight my blush, but nothing gets past Rach's sharp observational skills.

She sniggers. "Good for you. I'm glad you're happy."

"I am. I mean, I still miss my parents, and there are times when a memory surges to the forefront of my mind and I'm unbelievably sad and overcome with grief, but I know they'd want me to be happy, to move on with my life."

"Have you visited the graveyard yet?"

I swallow the painful lump in my throat as I nod. "I've been a couple of times. Ky is coming with me tomorrow." The previous times I visited I asked him to wait outside, but now I want him to *meet* my parents.

"I'm glad you have him. He's good for you."

"He is. I'm so happy." I pour a glass of wine as I smile over Rach's head at a couple of guys I know. "What about you? Any man on the scene?"

She shakes her head. "Nah. You know me." She takes a big glug of her drink. I've known Rachel since I was thirteen, and she's never had a steady boyfriend. I don't understand it. She's drop-dead-gorgeous, and dudes are falling all over her, but she knocks each and every one back. I can't understand how she'd rather hook up and indulge in one-night stands rather than find someone she cares about. Not that I'm judging. If guys can do it, then so can girls, and it doesn't mean that Rachel is a slut, because she isn't. She's still picky over who she hooks up with.

"Why not?" I pin her with a serious look.

"Why not what?" Jill asks, materializing in the kitchen sans Sam. She takes the chilled bottle of wine from the fridge and pours herself a large glass.

"I'm just asking Rach why she isn't going out with anyone."

"Don't bother," Jill drawls. "You won't get an honest answer out of that one." She sends a pointed look at Rach, and Rach scowls at her.

"Don't judge what you don't know!" Rach hisses.

I don't know what the hell has happened with these two since I left Ireland, but there's definite friction, and it's evident every time I've been in their company. It makes me sad. We were thick as thieves during our teenage years, and I thought our bond of friendship would never die. Jill first alluded to this when the girls visited me in Massachusetts last November, and I felt instantly guilty, sure my absence in their lives had somehow contributed to the situation, but since I've been back in Ireland, I've realized it's more than that. I hate that there's a wedge between them.

"No one is judging you, Rach," I say softly, trying to defuse the awkward atmosphere. "I just want you to be happy."

"Happiness is an illusion." She drains her G&T and begins preparing another one. Jill's brows knit together as she looks at me. "Or a luxury I cannot afford."

I place my hand on her arm. "I wish you'd tell us."

She shrugs, keeping her eyes fixed on the counter. "There's nothing to tell." Jill shakes her head sadly. I know she's worried about her, but her patience is wearing thin. It's obvious something is up with Rach, but she doesn't seem predisposed to share. While I can bide my time until she's ready to open up, Jill is increasingly frustrated at what she feels is a deception on Rach's part. She doesn't understand why Rach can't just tell her what's wrong, and it's tearing them apart.

Rach has always kept her cards close to her chest, so it's not really anything new. When I first moved to Dublin and met the girls, I was so consumed in my own problems that I didn't notice anything was up with Rach for ages. When I did cop it, I asked her if she wanted to talk and she deflected. She's been doing it ever since.

But I get it.

I understand, and I will never be the type to push her on it. Not when I spent years trapped in my own head, dealing with crap I had no control over. If anyone understands how difficult it is to manage stuff like that, it's me. And I know you can't force the feelings to come out. Sharing is difficult, yet also cathartic, but the timing has to be right. It can't be rushed or forced.

Over the last couple of years, I've reminded her I'm here for her and tentatively suggested therapy. It's helped me enormously, and it most likely would help her too, but she seems reluctant to take that step.

The doorbell goes off again, and Jill seizes the opportunity to escape. Rach turns back around, swirling her drink with her finger. There's a petulant look on her face. I nudge her shoulder. "Chill. We just worry about you."

"You shouldn't. I'm fine."

I clink her glass with mine. "Cool. I hope you know I'm always here for you if you ever want to talk."

Her shoulders visibly relax. "Thanks. I know that, and you're a good friend, Faye." Her eyes turn shiny. "If I was going to tell anyone, it'd be you," she whispers, and my breath hitches in my throat. It's the first time she's come close to acknowledging there is something. "I really miss you."

Her voice chokes a little, and a deep pain pierces my chest cavity. I hate that she's hurting and I'm seemingly powerless to do anything about it. I'm just about to tell her I miss her too when another familiar voice rings out across the room.

"Wow!" Luke whistles none too discreetly, his eyes raking me from head to toe. "Faye, you look fucking gorgeous." He holds out his arms in invitation. "Come here, baby. I've missed you."

Chapter Two

Kyler

I walk into the kitchen and stop dead in my tracks. Some douchebag has Faye locked in a tight embrace, his hands resting on the top of her ass. Her back is facing me, so I have a perfect view of the lovelorn expression on his face. "You smell fucking gorgeous, too." He leers, and I stalk toward them with my fists clenched at my side. His hand creeps up her back, winding into her hair as she struggles to remove herself from his grasp.

"Get your fucking hands off her." My growl and my expression are predatory in the extreme, and I couldn't give a shit. The jerk needs to know she's mine. I'm about two seconds away from knocking this asshole flat on his back.

His head picks up, and his eyes narrow as he stares at me. Faye manages to wriggle out of his embrace. Her hands land on my chest as I continue glaring at the douche. "Babe, it's okay. He doesn't mean anything by it." She turns and levels one of her deadly looks at the guy. "Isn't that right, Luke?"

Luke? Shit. Now I know who he is. He's her ex. Who clearly wishes he wasn't if the drunken lusty look in his eyes is any indication.

"Who the hell are you?" he demands, eyeballing me with ill-disguised venom.

"I'm Kyler. Faye's *boyfriend*." I enunciate the word, wrapping my arm possessively around her shoulder.

He snorts, and my nostrils flare. "Fuck me. It's true?" He pins Faye with a skeptical look. "You're screwing your cousin? For real?"

Faye turns rigid beside me, and a muscle ticks in her jaw. "I'm only telling you this out of respect for what we shared in the past," she says through gritted teeth. "Ky is my cousin by marriage only. There are no blood ties and nothing stopping us from dating, or screwing, as you so politely put it. So, in answer to your question, yes, I'm happily screwing my cousin, and I'm going to continue screwing my cousin for as long as he wants me."

"I still love you, baby," Luke slurs, completely ignoring me. *Didn't he hear what she just said?* What an idiot. Then again, if I ever lost her, I would probably act the exact same way. A bout of intense shivers whips up and down my spine at that hideous thought. I force it aside, inwardly chastising myself for even thinking such a thing. We are together forever, and I'm never letting her go.

Never.

"No, you don't. You're drunk, and if you only came here to stir shit, you know where the door is." Faye points behind her. "I mean it, Luke. I don't want to throw you out, but I will if I have to. I'm with Ky now, and I won't have you upsetting him in my own home."

"I'm in love with Faye and you need to back the hell off," I add, just so the douche gets the message loud and clear.

"Or what?" he snarls, stepping up.

He's as tall as me so I'm looking directly into his eyes when I reply. "Or my fist will make you."

He barks out a laugh, and three other guys move into position behind him. I release Faye, flexing my knuckles. I'm confident I can get a few punches in before they overwhelm me.

"I don't think so, *yank*." His lips curve into a sneer. "I don't know what you've done to corrupt my girl, but she's clearly not thinking straight."

My girl? What a delusional jerk. *How did Faye ever go out with this idiot?* Then again, I'm hardly in any position to throw stones. I dated that psycho Addison.

Faye mumbles incoherently under her breath as I grab his shirt. "Listen here, asshole. She's mine. She'll always be mine, so do us all a favor and fuck off."

Rach puts her drink down on the counter and steps forward, nudging her way in between us. She plants one hand on each of us. "Cool the jets, boys. There'll be no fighting on my watch. Capiche?" She sends daggers at both of us, and I'd challenge any guy not to cower under the weight of her impressive glare. She turns her death ray on the guys behind Luke. "Same goes for you idiots. Fuck off unless you can control yourselves. I mean it."

"Aw, come on, Rach. There's no need to be like that," the beefy, dark-haired guy says.

"Shut your gob, Conor. I'm not taking any of your shite tonight."

He winks at her, and she gives him the middle finger. The other guys chuckle, and the tension evaporates.

"Get your hand off me," Luke demands, grabbing Rachel's wrist.

I pull her to my side, shielding her with my body as I peer into his pissed-off face. "What is it with you and touching girls without their permission?"

"I've known them for years. You're just a blow in. Quit telling me what to do." He puffs his chest out, and the urge to pummel him into next week is riding me hard.

Faye sighs. "Right, that's it." She takes Luke's elbow. "Bye, bye, Luke. Off you go." She drags him toward the door.

His eyes pop wide. "You're kicking me out? *Me?*"

"Yep. There's way too much testosterone in the air for my liking, and I've had enough of you insulting my boyfriend. Maybe I'll see you around before I leave." She shrugs, and his shoulders slump a bit.

"When did you become so stuck up? I remember what you told me, you know. You said tha—"

Rachel clamps a hand over his mouth and starts hauling him away. "That's enough out of you." She swats the back of his head. "You're an idiot."

"And you're still a mean drunk," he slurs ironically.

She shoves him out the door, and his posse trails behind, shooting me a few choice looks as they go.

"Well, that was entertaining," Jill pipes up rather cheerily from her position at the far wall. She's leaning back against her boyfriend. Sam has his arms around her waist and his chin on her shoulder. They're a nice couple and I've enjoyed hanging out with them. There's no drama and that's refreshing.

Sam locks eyes with me, grinning. "Luke's always had a thing for Faye, but he's harmless really. And it's not like you've got anything to worry about."

I pull two beers from the refrigerator, tossing one to him. "Faye knows I'm the jealous type. Can't help it even if I trust her more than I've ever trusted anyone."

"Don't be jealous." She circles her arms around my waist from behind. "No one else could ever compare to you."

Just like that, my sour mood disappears. Rachel makes a gagging sound from behind, and I turn us as one, grinning like a fool.

She mock pouts, reaching for her drink. "I'm surrounded by lovesick couples. It's disgusting, and it's turning my stomach."

"Well, if you're looking for a little action, the rest of my brothers arrive next week." I send her a suggestive wink while Faye slaps the back of my head. "Ow." I rub the sore spot. "What was that for?"

"Don't be encouraging that."

Rach and I both turn dirty looks on Faye, and she holds up her hands.

"Are you insinuating my brothers aren't good enough for your best friend?" I quirk a brow.

"Are you insinuating *I'm* not good enough for your cousins?" Rachel plants her hands on her hips, leveling a slightly hurt look at her friend.

"I'm not insinuating anything of the sort, and there's no need to look so hurt. I couldn't care less if you hooked up with any of my cousins. It's just, I thought you were anti-men these days, and if you want to avoid complications, you should definitely steer clear."

Rach almost chokes on her drink. "Anti-boyfriend does not mean anti-men. As if!" She huffs jokingly.

"You can expect Kent to be all over you," I explain, remembering how his disastrous attempts at flirting with her last year were immediately shot down. Kent loves a challenge, and he's not one to back down easily. Rejection barely makes a dent in his confidence.

"I'm looking for a man not a boy."

"Ouch. I suggest you don't mention that to his face." I'm not sure even Kent's uber-confidence could withstand that put-down.

"Are your older brothers still single?"

I tip some beer into my mouth before replying. "I honestly couldn't tell you, but I'll find out."

"Okay, Mr. Wannabe Matchmaker," Faye says, pinching my butt. "I think that's enough interference from you. Rach is well capable of making all the necessary moves."

"Too right, girlfriend," Rachel says, high-fiving Faye. "And right now we're going to make some other moves." Faye's forehead puckers in confusion. Rachel laughs. "We're dancing. Come on." Then she grabs my girlfriend, dragging her into the midst of the writhing crowd in the living room.

The rest of the party passes by uneventfully, and we finally crawl into bed at five a.m. when the last of the stragglers have left. Jill and Sam went to bed at around two, and Rachel passed out about an hour ago. I helped Faye carry her to the other spare bedroom.

I slip into the bed, curling my naked body around Faye, chuckling at her light snoring. She's already out for the count, and it doesn't take me long to follow suit.

The next morning, I rise early, cooking a big breakfast for everyone. Smells of coffee and bacon draw the others to the kitchen, and we reminisce about the night as we chat in between eating. Rachel is very quiet this morning, but I figure she's nursing the mother of all hangovers. I pour her a second cup of black coffee without asking. She accepts it from me with a grateful smile. Her big brown eyes are sad as she stares into the swirling liquid, and not for the first time I wonder what's happened to her. I've had enough personal demons to recognize them in others. Still, it's none of my business. But she's a nice girl, and I hate to see her in pain. I hope whatever is bothering her gets resolved soon.

After breakfast, we walk our friends to the front door. "I'll call you during the week," Faye says, hugging the girls goodbye.

"What day do your brothers get here?" Rachel asks, giving me a quick hug.

"Next Saturday."

"I'm going to throw them a 'welcome to Ireland' party that night. Unless you've already made plans?"

I smile at her. "Nope. We were just planning on crashing here before Mom forces us into all the touristy shit she's lined up, so that's perfect. I'm sure they'd love that."

"Great. That's sorted." She beams, pushing strands of her long brunette hair back off her face.

"You sure your parents won't mind?" Faye asks, looping her arm in mine.

"They're still abroad, and I have the house to myself. They won't care."

"Okay, then. Thanks, babe." Faye hugs her again. "Call me if you need any help with the party planning."

"Will do!" She waves as she runs out, hopping into the back seat of Sam's car.

I clean up the kitchen while Faye gets ready. "You sure you still want to do this?" she asks, coming into the kitchen looking all cute in her jean shorts and tight white tank top. A pink cardigan is wrapped around her toned stomach, and she's wearing black Converse. My eyes travel a path up her long, slim, tanned legs, and blood rushes south. I discreetly adjust myself in my jeans, and her lips purse knowingly.

Grinning, I reel her into my arms, unable to resist touching her. "Yes." I kiss the tip of her nose. "Unless you've changed your mind?"

She kisses me softly. "No. I want you to come with."

I grab my hoodie off the back of the chair, lacing my hand in hers. "Okay, then. Let's go."

♥♥♥♥♥♥♥

The graveyard is only a twenty-minute drive from Faye's house. I grasp her hand firmly in mine as we walk through the vast cemetery. Glorious sunshine beats down on us making a mockery of everything I've ever heard about Ireland. It rained for about an hour the first Wednesday we were here, but every other day has been sunny and dry. Faye joked we brought the good weather with us. We nod at an elderly man as he passes by, leaning on a curved walking cane for support. There isn't anyone else in sight on this side of the humongous graveyard. Faye veers right, tugging me along a row that is under the protective shade of towering oak trees that look as old as dirt.

She stops in front of two adjoining graves with matching marble headstones. Clinging tightly to my hand, she gulps, smiling nervously. She bends down, removing the dried, withered flowers in front of both graves, replacing them with the fresh ones we bought at the cemetery gate.

Dropping down on her butt, she crosses her legs in front of her, and I mirror her position. "Hey, Mum. Hi, Dad. As promised, I brought Ky to meet you."

Pushing aside my discomfort, I clear my throat. "Hey, Mr. and Mrs. Donovan, I'm Kyler, and I'm madly in love with your daughter." Faye laughs quietly, and I run my fingers through her hair. "Thank you for raising such a beautiful, smart, sexy woman." She leans into me, kissing my cheek. "I wish I'd had the opportunity to meet you in person, and it sucks that your passing was the event that brought Faye into my life. I like to think we would've met any way because she's the only girl for me." My voice turns soft, and a tear gleams in Faye's eye. I twist my head around, focusing on the headstone. "I want you to know that I'll take really good care of her. You don't need to worry. She has me, and I'll be by her side for as long as she'll have me." A strangled sob rips from Faye's lips, and I tuck her in under my arm, kissing her temple. "I will love her, protect her, and support her for the rest of my days. I give you my solemn promise."

A gentle breeze ghosts over my skin, and the trees that line the perimeter of the cemetery swish back and forth, creating an eerie but peaceful ambience. Faye sniffles, and I hold her tighter. Her arms wrap firmly around my waist, and I press a kiss to her hair, closing my eyes as I inhale the familiar smell of vanilla and lavender. The smell that I now associate with home.

"Words cannot convey how much I love you, Ky," she whispers a few minutes later. "You make everything better. You don't know how much it means that you came here with me, that you said that." She sniffles again, and I hand her a tissue from my pocket.

"I meant every word, babe."

"I know."

I tilt her chin up, peering intently into her glassy eyes. "I will always be here for you. No matter what. My world would cease to exist if you weren't in it, and that's not something I'll ever consider. I'm going to propose to you one day, Faye." I kiss the back of her hand. "I want marriage, kids, everything, with you."

She beams, and a shy blush spreads over her face. "I want that too, babe. There isn't anyone more perfect for me."

I kiss the tip of her nose. "Thank fuck. You mean the world to me, Faye. There isn't anything I wouldn't do for you."

She sighs, and her features relax. "God, if I could bottle you, I'd make a fortune!"

Her comment breaks the heavy emotion in the air, and we both laugh. "Ditto, baby," I say, pecking her lips. "Absolutely, ditto."

Chapter Three

Faye

The rest of the week passes by in a whirlwind. I drag Ky everywhere, but he doesn't complain. We took the Dart to Sandycove one day to go swimming. The weather was fab, and we had a lazy day swimming and sunbathing between Sandycove and Killiney Beach. Another day was spent in Dublin city center, shopping up a storm and then drinking and dancing into the early hours. Ky still can't get over the fact he can legally drink in bars and clubs, and we might have overdone it a bit, having to drag ourselves out of bed with matching sore heads the next day.

I've deliberately held off on the usual touristy stuff because I know Alex and James want us to do all that the first few days they are here, but I did take him to Croke Park to see Leinster beat Munster in the All Ireland GAA quarter finals, and we did the Skyline walk so I could show him all the key landmarks in the capital city. We spent a couple of nights hanging with Sam, Jill, and Rachel, but I'm glad we have tonight to ourselves and that we're staying in. The rest of the Kennedy gang arrives tomorrow, and I just want to enjoy our last night alone.

"Here." Ky hands me a large bowl of popcorn, flopping down on the couch beside me. "Have you found something to watch?"

I show him a couple of movie options on Netflix, and he picks a horror that neither of us has seen yet. I spend most of the time with my face buried in his shoulder while he chuckles and calls me a scaredy cat. The knots in my shoulders only loosen when the credits roll, and I stretch my limbs, pleased to have gotten through the ordeal in one piece. A loud yawn slips out of my mouth when Ky gets up to flick the light back on. "You tired, babe? I don't mind an early night."

My eyes narrow, and I survey him through hooded eyes.

He laughs, throwing himself down on top of me on the couch. "What?" He puts on an innocent face, but his eyes twinkle with mischief.

"Somehow I think your version of an early night and mine are at completely opposite ends of the spectrum."

"You have a one-track mind."

"Says the person whose hands are currently sliding up my body."

He looks down at his offending hands, which are half under my T-shirt, edging dangerously close to the underside of my bra. A perplexed look washes over his face. "How did they get there?"

I roll my eyes. "Are you trying to tell me your wandering hands have a mind of their own?"

His fingers creep over the curve of one breast, slipping into my bra and caressing the skin there. An ache starts building down below. "Shit! This isn't me. Swear. I'm not doing this, like at all." His words of protest are shot to pieces by the wide smirk on his face.

"You think you're funny, huh?" I remove his hand from my boob, attempting to wriggle out from under him. When that doesn't work, I switch to Plan B, moving my foot up and over the bulge in his jeans. "You won't be laughing when I bring you to the brink and then fall asleep."

"You wouldn't dare."

"Try me."

He mock pouts before his expression turns softly serious. "If you're not in the mood, that's totally fine. I was only messing around." His hand slithers down my body and he lifts off me.

"It's not that." I shake my head. He sits up straight, hoisting me into his lap. "It's never ever that." I kiss him sweetly. "You know how much I love sex with you, but we should really speak about tomorrow first."

His muscles tense up beneath me. "I don't want to discuss it again. This is our last night alone, and I don't want to spend it arguing."

I place my hands on his shoulders and peer into his beautiful blue eyes. "I don't either, but we haven't resolved it, and I can't relax if I think you're going to tell him."

He leans back, pulling me with him, until we're lying down with me curled into his side. He sighs as his hand runs lightly up and down my back. "We promised no more secrets or lies."

"I know, but that's between us. I've told you now and explained why I didn't say anything before. Why can't that be enough?"

"Because he's my brother, Faye, and I think he has a right to know."

"It's not our place to make that call."

"Considering what Lana did to Kal, I don't see how the fuck she gets to call the shots," he snaps.

I prop up on an elbow as familiar frustration bubbles to the surface. "It's her life, Ky, and she made me promise. I *promised* I wouldn't tell him I've been in regular contact with her, and I'm not going back on my word."

"You shouldn't have made that fucking promise." A muscle pops in his jaw as he glares at me. "Where exactly do your loyalties lie?"

That incenses me no end, and I jump up off the couch, glowering at him as I prod his chest with my finger. "I can't believe you've asked me that! You know damn well where my loyalties lie! I'm trying to do the right thing, and I believe letting destiny take its course is the best thing to do. That way we're not influencing anything, and if they are meant to reconnect, they will!"

He sits bolt upright, resting his head in his hands. "Do not throw that destiny crap into the mix."

Red rage infiltrates my veins, inflaming every cell, nerve ending, and tissue. "Now destiny is crap?" My voice is intentionally low. "Is what we have crap?"

He whips his head up. "Stop twisting my words. You know I didn't mean it like that."

"I fucking hate double standards!" I yell. "And that's exactly what this is." I start pacing the carpet, silently cursing Lana for putting me in this predicament.

He stands up, anger blazing in his eyes. "All I'm asking is that you think about this logically! Kal is enrolled in UF and he has a right to know Lana is going there too."

"He already knows, Ky! Why the hell do you think he changed his plans and enrolled there? He's done that for her!"

He throws his hands into the air. "Then what's the problem in telling him we know she's going there? You're talking in fucking riddles."

I stalk toward him, pushing my finger into his chest again. "Because *she* doesn't know he's going there! And if I tell him, then he'll want her number, and I promised. I *promised* her I wouldn't pass it on. If Kal wanted us involved he would've been honest in explaining why he's switched to UF, but he's deliberately feeding us a pack of lies about their architecture program, blah, blah. *He* doesn't want to involve us, *she* doesn't want to involve us, so we shouldn't be involved!" I shriek, anger getting the better of me.

Ky opens and shuts his mouth, and we stand off, glaring at one another as hostile emotions fuel the air between this. I hate this. I hate that it's coming between us, and I'm torn in two. I hate that I'm concealing this from my cousin, but the other side of my brain believes this is the best course of action. If they are meant to be together, it should happen naturally, not because Ky and I played matchmaker.

"You're asking me to lie to my brother," Ky says more calmly than I would have expected. "How can I be okay with that?" A look of pure anguish is written on his face. I don't have a response because it's the truth, and it doesn't sit right with me either. On more than one occasion in the last three weeks, I've considered phoning Lana and telling her, but I've held back because I wouldn't put it past her to react adversely.

"Ky, I know I'm asking for a lot." Tentatively, I touch his arm, pleased when his fingers curl around mine instead of pushing me away. "I know I'm asking you to trust me blind in the understanding that I could be calling this completely wrong. I don't want to lie to Kal either, but I also don't want to get his hopes up unfairly. He loves her. If I tell him she's going there, if I confirm it, he'll want her number because he'll want to ring her straightaway. If I don't give it to him, he'll just get Kev to hack into my phone. If he rings her, he might scare her away, and then he'll lose her forever. Is that what you want for him?"

"Maybe it'll give him the closure he needs."

I shake my head. "He doesn't want closure, Ky. He wants *her*. Why else do you think he's going to college in Florida? He's going because he wants her back in his life."

"How can he want her after what she did?" He curls a hand around my neck, drawing me slowly against his body. "I don't understand it."

I shrug. "The heart wants who it wants. And he knows that her actions were driven by grief and hurt not by any real intent."

"It doesn't excuse what she did."

"I know that, but she's genuinely remorseful, and look at what she did to try and make amends. The media destroyed her rep, Ky. She could have retracted her statement quietly, but she chose to do it publicly to ensure his reputation was scrubbed clean. She did that because she loves him."

"You're clearly more compassionate than me."

I cup his face. "You grew up with Lana too. Is she a horrible person?"

"No, but I'm not sure the Lana we grew up with is the same girl."

I shrug again. "None of us are the same, and we've all made our fair share of mistakes. And it's not about me having more compassion." I chew on my lower lip. "I've given it a lot of thought. What if that had been us? What if it was me who had falsely accused you? Would you stop loving me? Stop wanting me? Would you give up if I took off and just move on with your life?"

He is quietly contemplative, before slowly shaking his head. "You know I wouldn't do that."

I nod. "And I wouldn't either. And we don't have the kind of history they have."

Ky rests his forehead against mine, exhaling deeply. I wrap my arms around his waist. This is an impossible situation, and I hate that it's been a source of ongoing conflict between us this entire trip. "Okay. We'll do it your way. I won't say anything to him."

Air whooshes out of my lungs. "Thank you. And if it goes pear-shaped, I'll take all the blame."

He eases back, grasping my face in his hands. "No, you won't. We've decided this together, and if it blows up in our faces, we'll accept the responsibility together."

The following afternoon, we travel to Dublin airport with Rachel and Jill to greet the rest of the family. Ky is giving us girls a wide berth as we jostle for prime space in front of the arrivals gate. Jill was up half the night making a massive "Ireland welcomes the Kennedys" banner complete with vibrant hand-drawn pictures and multicolored glitter. She's super proud of her work of art and happily brandishing it about. *It's a little cringey, but what kind of friend would I be if I didn't enter into the spirit of things?* Ky is hanging back, afraid it'll offend his masculinity or something.

They're traveling by commercial jet this time, which surprised me, although it'll be first class all the way.

Jill emits a sudden shriek, enthusiastically waving the banner and lifting it so high it's blocking my view. I tug it down to chest level so I can see.

Alex is leading the posse as they step out through the sliding doors, and, honestly, it's like watching a trailer for the latest hot boys' movie. A quiet hush settles over the place as my cousins saunter toward the exit like bona fide movie stars. Time seems to freeze as they walk toward us in slow-mo. They are all wearing jeans and tight-fitting T-shirts showcasing glistening tanned skin and buff, toned, muscular physiques. Not a hair is out of place when Keanu takes up the lead, strutting in long strides as if he's on the catwalk. Keaton has a customary cheeky grin on his face, while Kent is sporting the usual smug look. Kaden's sharp eyes examine his surroundings without giving anything away. Spotting us, Kal sends me a cheeky wink, gracing us with a beaming smile. With a duffel bag thrown casually over his shoulder, Keven walks alongside my uncle. Sporting dark shades, a shorter crew cut, and bigger biceps which flex and roll as he walks, highlighting the edge of his tattoo, he looks totally badass. James waves, and I wave back as a surge of excitement whittles through me. I've really enjoyed my three weeks here with Ky, but I'm so looking forward to this next leg of our trip.

Several jaws drop in the vicinity. and you can almost hear the collective female gasp. "Ho. Lee. Shit," Rachel whispers. "Talk about stage presence."

I giggle. "I know. Ireland isn't going to know what's hit them."

"Who is the one walking beside your uncle? I still get so confused over all their names."

"That's Keven. We met him and Kaden that afternoon in Harvard. Remember?"

Recognition lights up her eyes. "He didn't look quite so fit back then."

She must've been blind. Kev's always sported that ripped look. I nudge her in the ribs. "Want me to ask Ky to get the lowdown on his love life?"

She wets her lips. "Yes, please."

We share a grin just as Alex and Keanu step around the corner. Alex rushes Ky, wrapping him in an enormous hug. You'd swear she hadn't seen him in three years, not just three weeks. I walk over to them and find myself enveloped in her arms. "Sweetheart. It's so good to see you both. And you too, girls," she says over my head to Jill and Rach. "We're so excited to be here!"

"Where's the bar?" Kent asks, looking around.

"Missed you too, you little shit." Ky slaps him on the back. "And you're only sixteen, so there'll be no bar for the likes of you."

"Screw off, assface. I'll be seventeen in a few months, and everyone knows we look older." It's hard to argue against Kent's statement. The triplets have shed that baby-faced look, and with their sharp, chiseled good looks, buff bodies, and looming six-foot-plus height, I think most people would automatically assume they're of age. Not that it matters much here. Underage drinking isn't anything unusual, and it's not that difficult to get drink if you're so inclined.

"Kent, please. We've only just landed, and we already talked about this," James says, looking up at the ceiling and sighing.

Kent's eyes narrow as he spots Rach, and he makes a beeline for her. "Hey, babe." He winks. "Fancy meeting you here." He waggles his brows, and I try not to throw up.

"Kent." Her tone is polite but not overly friendly. "I hope you have a good holiday." Before he can get another word in, she smiles quickly and walks toward Alex.

James reaches over, pulling Ky and me into a group hug. "How are you two? How's the trip been so far?"

Ky slides his arm around my waist, smiling as he peers into my eyes. "Incredible. We're having an amazing time. Faye has dragged me everywhere this week, but it's been good."

"I'm surprised you even stepped foot outside the front door," Kal pipes up, leaning in to hug me.

"Funny, ha!" I lightly punch him in the arm.

"What's up, asshole?" Ky asks, slapping Kal on the back.

I dart over to Keaton, squealing as I wrap my arms around him. "I can't believe you're here! We're going to have the best time ever."

He lifts me up, twirling me around as if I weigh nothing. "Me either! I drove everyone insane on the plane because I was so hyped up."

"Truth," Kaden says, coming over. "He's lucky we didn't throw him out the emergency door." When Keaton sets my feet on the ground, Kaden gives me a quick one-armed hug. "Good to see you, cuz."

"You too."

"Faye." Keven stands back a bit, jerking his head in my direction.

"Hey, Kev." I work hard to keep my eyes on his face. It's monumentally difficult with those biceps which just beg to be ogled.

"Hi," Rach says, pushing her way forward. "I'm Rachel. We met last year."

"Of course. I remember." Taking off his shades, he smiles as he makes a slow perusal of her body. She practically melts into a puddle at his feet.

Ky chuckles under his breath, moving behind me and circling his arms around my waist. "I don't think she'll be needing my services after all."

"Nope. She's got this one covered." I smirk.

"Hi, Ky, Faye. How's it going?" Keanu says, stepping in front of us.

"Hey. I'm glad we could tear you away from Selena for a few weeks."

"I'm my own person, Faye," he retorts, scowling a little.

Ky musses up his perfectly styled hair, and his scowl deepens. "Chill, bro. She's only messing with ya."

"I think we should make a move," James suggests. "We're blocking the entrance." I look behind him, and sure enough, a queue is forming as people struggle to maneuver around us.

"That guy over there is for you," Ky supplies, pointing at a small, bald man in a gray suit standing off to the side with a KENNEDY PARTY sign clutched to his chest. "I drove my rental, so I'll drive back to Faye's, and then we'll meet you at the hotel for dinner."

"Sounds like a plan." James beams proudly at Ky. "See you in a while."

Chapter Four

Kyler

Rach and Jill join us in the hotel for dinner, and it's a lively affair. All my brothers are itching to get the party started, so we leave Mom and Dad to their own devices and take a couple of taxis to Rachel's house.

She has hired help to set up the party, so we kick back the minute we get there while we wait for everyone else to arrive.

Kev is totally checking Rachel out, not even attempting to disguise his interest. She's frothing at the mouth, and I give it one hour, tops, before one of them pounces on the other. When she visited last year, I could've sworn it was Brad who snagged her attention. The way those two baited each other spoke volumes. I have a sneaky suspicion that something happened between them, but if anything went down, Brad kept it to himself.

Thoughts of my best friend raise the usual snowstorm of emotions. Brad should be on this trip—he's practically one of the family—and it doesn't feel right he was left behind on his lonesome. But if he'd come, it would've ruined the vacation for everyone. There's no hiding the awkward tension that lingers in the air like rotten eggs whenever Brad, me, and Faye share the same space.

It's one of the reasons Faye and I have decided to live apart when we get to Harvard. Initially, I'd assumed we would get a place together, and I was pissed when she first suggested we live separately, but once she explained her reasoning, I got over it. She wants the full college experience, and that means dorm life. So, she's going to share with a roomie, and Brad and I are going to share an apartment a few blocks from campus. I lined up a place before I left home so everything's all set. I'm hoping this year will give me and Brad the chance to get our friendship back on track. I'm praying he meets some girl and gets over his obsession with Faye.

While Faye hasn't outright admitted she's hoping for the same things, I know she is. I don't know what part it played in her decision to stay on campus, but I can't fault her for trying to repair the friendship between Brad and me. I only love her more for her selflessness. Ultimately, that's what decided it for me. If she can selflessly sacrifice getting our own place, then I can do the same for her. And it's not like we won't see each other. I'll still be tied to her like glue. I want to ensure all those a-holes on campus know she's taken.

Once a possessive jerk, always a possessive jerk. I chuckle to myself.

"Penny for them," Faye says, sliding alongside me. She hands me a fresh, cold beer.

"Thanks, babe." I peck her lips. "I was just thinking about Brad and Harvard."

"Yeah, me too." She quietly surveys the room which is starting to fill up. "It doesn't feel right he's not here."

"I know."

"I don't like the thoughts of him being back in the house all by himself."

"Me either, but there wasn't really an alternative."

Little lines furrow her brow, and her expression turns sad. "No, I don't suppose there was."

I tilt her face up to mine. "It's not your fault," I say for like the umpteenth time.

"I should never have kissed him."

A growl rips from my soul. "Can we not talk about this? There's no point rehashing old ground. It'll only ruin both of our moods, and I want to enjoy the party."

She grips my waist tightly, reeling me in closer. "You're right. No more talk of the past. Now shut up and kiss me."

I drag Faye over to the corner of the room, dropping into a leather chair and pulling her into my lap. Then I kiss the hell out of her, allowing her familiar touch to ease the tightness in my chest.

"Still horny as fuck I see," Kal says, breaking us apart. He's leaning against the wall with Keaton by his side, grinning knowingly.

"Shut it, asshole." I discreetly adjust myself as Faye launches off my lap. She pulls me up, smiling like I'm her favorite person in the world. *Is it arrogant that I know I am?* She smooths a hand down the front of her dress, and my eyes greedily follow the movement.

"Fucking hell, Ky," Kal moans. "I'd forgotten how nauseating it is to be around you guys sometimes. Haven't you had your fill by now?"

"Dude, that day will never come."

"Aw, you say the sweetest things." Faye leans in to kiss my cheek. "I'm going to check in with Rach. I'll be back in a sec." She pecks my lips before leaving.

"I think it's awesome you guys are so much in love," Keaton says with an envious look on his face.

I clink my bottle against his. "Thanks, bro. You still seeing Melissa?"

"Yeah," he confirms with little enthusiasm.

"What? It's on the outs?"

He stiffens. "I didn't say that. It's just..."

I arch a brow. "What?"

A crooked smile spreads over his mouth. "We're going to talk girls and love and shit?"

I shrug. "If you want to."

His smile widens. "You've changed."

I think about that for a minute. "Yeah, I think I have. Faye has played no small part in that. You'll be the same when you meet the one." Kal has a faraway look on his face. I elbow him in the ribs. "What about you?"

He visibly stiffens. "What about me?" His tone is decidedly defensive.

"You haven't been with anyone in ages. We're on vacation. You should let loose." I skim an eye over the large crowd. "There's plenty of hot girls here. You should get back in the saddle."

A muscle clenches in his jaw. "I'm not interested."

Keaton and I lock eyes.

"You miss Lana," Keaton says quietly.

Kal looks at the floor. "I don't want to talk about it."

A layer of tension descends. What an awesome fucking start to the second leg of our vacation.

"Wow," Faye says returning a moment later. "I can't leave you alone for five minutes. Why the glum faces? This is a party, guys! It's supposed to be fun." She plants her hands on her hips as a cunning expression appears on her face. "Put your drinks down. We're dancing." Her stern tone says "don't even think about arguing with me."

She hauls the three of us out into the middle of the floor, where people are dancing up a storm. The place is jammed now, and there's got to be at least one hundred and fifty people milling about Rachel's living room. A DJ pumps out beats from the corner of the room, and the sounds of raucous laughter can be heard in the background.

Several girls focus their attention in our direction, and once Kent and Keanu join us, it isn't long before we are pretty much surrounded. Of course, Kade and Kev are too cool to join in, preferring to hang back, chatting to a few girls over on the other side of the room.

Kent lets out a roar when the latest Bieber hit belts out, whipping off his shirt and flinging it around as the girls move in for the kill. Grabbing his beer, he misses his mouth and ends up pouring it over his naked chest. A busty brunette and a tiny blonde are on him in a flash. My eyes are out on stalks as I watch them lick a path up and down his bare chest. Faye is cracking up laughing beside me, clutching her stomach as if in pain. "Oh my God. This is fucking priceless." Kent grinds against the two girls, happy to be the meat in their sandwich, and I don't need to be psychic to figure out how this is going to end. "Do not encourage him," I shout in her ear.

"Aw, come on, babe. You have to admit it's funny. I know those girls, and they are going to eat him alive." She giggles, moving in to hear whatever Keaton has to say. It's then I notice a red-haired girl grasping Keaton's ass as she attempts to eye fuck him. The panic on Keaton's face would be comical if it wasn't terrifyingly real. Where Keanu and Kent are smoothly skillful around women, Keaton is the complete opposite. Unwanted female attention scares the shit out of him. While Kent doesn't know the meaning of commitment, Keaton is fiercely loyal to Melissa, and he's most definitely out of his comfort zone with the clinger-on. I decide to help him out.

Moving over, I bend down, leaning in close to the redhead's ear. "He's taken, sweetheart, so I suggest you remove your hands from my brother's ass before you give him a coronary."

The girl's eyes light up as she stares at me with a hungry expression. In record time, her hands are off Keaton's ass and planted on my chest. Not even a second passes before Faye is on the case. "Back the hell off, Chloe. He's mine," she snaps at the girl, removing her hands from my body and planting herself protectively in front of me as if I can't handle myself which is fucking laughable. But I'm not mad. Far from it. I love when my girl's claws come out. I'm instantly hard, and I push my erection into Faye's back, letting her know how much she's turning me on. She leans back into me with a whimper.

"Please tell me one of them is single?" Chloe wails.

"Not on your life," Faye hisses. "My cousins are too good for the likes of you. And how did you even get in here? I'm pretty sure Rach doesn't know."

"You're such a bitch, Faye."

"You really don't want to go there. I'd suggest you leave before Rach makes you."

"Cow," she mutters, storming off.

"What was that all about?" I whisper in her ear.

"She has a well-founded rep for going after other girls' boyfriends, and she had a fling this one time with this guy Rach had been seeing. It's the closest Rach has ever come to going out with anyone, but she cut the guy loose when she found out he was also fooling around with Chloe."

"Can we take a breather?" Keaton asks, interrupting us, and we take pity on him. Kal goes to grab some drinks while we meander toward Kade and Kev.

"Okay, wow," Faye exclaims with wide eyes, pointing ahead. "Keven looks like he's going to consume Rach alive."

She isn't wrong. My brother has Faye's best friend pinned to the wall, his body pressed tight against hers, his hands locked on either side of her face as he kisses the shit out of her. Not that she looks like she's complaining. Her hands are digging into his shoulders as she arches against him.

"They're as bad as you two," Keanu quips, pulling up the rear as he wipes a sheen of sweat off his brow with the corner of his shirt.

"Where's the delinquent?" I ask.

"Where do you think?" He smirks.

I cuss under my breath.

"He can take care of himself," Kade says, noticing my unhappiness. "Stop worrying."

"Easy for you to say." Kade pretty much washed his hands of us once he went to college, and he's not up to speed on everything. Kent is screwing his way through some number of girls, and I can't help worrying he's going to get himself into serious trouble one of these days.

"It's okay, babe." Faye circles her arms around my neck. "I know those girls, and they can definitely handle him. He might have met his match for once." Then she lowers her mouth to mine, and every other thought flees my mind.

♥♥♥♥♥♥♥

We eventually got home sometime after four, so when the alarm goes off at eight, it feels like I've been asleep for all of five minutes. Faye moans, mumbling curses in a sleep-laced tone, burrowing her head under the pillow. I swat her butt. "Babe, we have to get up. You know my mom will turn up and drag us out of bed if we don't show up at the hotel on time."

She flips over onto her back, removing the pillow from her face. Tangled strands of chocolaty-brown hair hide her beautiful features. "This is torture, pure and simple," she groans, brushing the hair back off her face. "Your mother is a sadist."

I run my hand up the inside of her thigh. "She's been called worse." My hand creeps higher, brushing over the edge of her panties.

She gasps, and her eyes blaze with instant desire. I push the silky material aside, inching one finger inside her. Damn, she's already so wet. Her eyes dart to the clock. "Do we have time?" she croaks.

I rip my boxers off in one fluid movement. "For you? Always."

♥♥♥♥♥♥♥

We're twenty minutes late to the hotel, and a round of cheers and clapping greets us when we amble into the lobby. My brothers are slouched in plush armchairs, all looking like death warmed up. Glad to see we aren't the only ones suffering today.

"There you are," Mom says, yanking me into a hug. "I was just about to send out a search party."

"Sorry. We woke late," I lie.

Kent snorts. "As if, bro. We all know you were too busy boning Faye to turn up on time."

Mom closes her eyes, clasping a hand to her chest.

"Kent. Don't start with this crap," Dad pleads. "You promised us you were going to be on your best behavior."

He stands up, yawning as he stretches his arms out over his head. "How is telling the truth *not* being on my best behavior? Seriously, I just can't win." He shakes his head.

"Matching hickeys," Faye cuts in, squinting as she examines either side of his neck. "So classy."

Every Kennedy head turns in Kent's direction, and a chorus of taunts ring out as all the attention is diverted his way. Faye smirks.

Round one to my girlfriend.

Chapter Five

Faye

Alex had asked me to email her a list of the main touristy things to do in Dublin a few weeks ago, and now I know why. She has an action-packed itinerary worked out for today and the next two days. On Wednesday, we are driving to Cork, and from there we'll move on to Kerry. Then, next weekend, we're traveling to Wexford to spend the week with Adam and my half-brothers, and I will also be meeting my grandparents for the first time. The thought still raises mixed emotions in me, and I'm in that nervous-excited space.

Really, Alex should have allocated more time in Dublin because she is trying to squeeze far too much into too short of a timeframe. She dragged us all over the city today. We visited The Guinness Storehouse, Kilmainham Gaol, The National Wax Museum, the Irish Whiskey Museum, and we even took a stroll through Temple Bar, stopping for a pint and dinner in one of the many pubs that line Dublin's notorious tourist district.

My feet are aching by the time Ky and I make it back to the house, but there's no time to dwell on it. We have one hour before we are due to meet his brothers in the city for a night of drinking and dancing—and if Kent has his way, no doubt, debauchery.

"I think I'm going to need a holiday after this holiday," I joke, stepping out of the bathroom, wrapped in a towel, with my wet hair dripping down my back. Ky is already dressed and ready to go. His tight, short-sleeved black shirt hugs his muscular frame in all the right places. He has the top two buttons undone, offering a glimpse of tanned, toned, and glistening skin. Dark jeans and black sneakers complete the look. His hair is still styled long on top and shorn into a skin fade at the sides. A layer of stubble lines his chiseled jawline, and the scent of his aftershave wafts through the air. He looks good enough to eat, and a familiar hunger steals over me.

His eyes smolder with desire when he notices my expression. "We can't be late again," he growls, his voice thick with lust. "My brothers will never let me hear the end of it." Unexpectedly, he drops to his knees in front of me. "But there's enough time to take care of you." He yanks the towel down my body, and I'm standing naked before him as his mouth moves to the place where I ache most for him. I gasp as I stumble a little, thrusting my hands out and gripping the edge of my dresser. Throwing back my head, I whimper as his tongue does unmentionable things to me. He devours me with his mouth and his tongue, and it's embarrassing how quickly I fall over that blissful ledge. He stays with me, milking every last drop of my arousal until I'm sated.

Standing up, he pulls me into a tender embrace. "I love you," he whispers, pressing a kiss to the top of my damp hair.

My arms snake around him, and I press my cheek to his chest, reveling in the smell and the feel of him. "I love you too."

I reach for him, but his hand grips my wrist. "We don't have time unless you're planning to go out naked, and if you are, then we need to have words."

I look up at him. "I can get ready super fast."

He kisses my mouth with glossy lips. "I'll take a rain check. Don't rush. Take your time. I fixed you a vodka and cranberry. It's by the bed."

"You're too good to me." I stretch up on tiptoes and kiss him. "And I'll make it up to you later."

He swats my butt as he makes his way out of my bedroom. "Hell, yeah, you will."

The Halo arrives a half hour later, just as I'm putting the finishing touches to my outfit. I'm wearing a black, silky jumpsuit, with a cut-out design on the back, and sky-high heels. My hair is pulled back in a slick ponytail, and my makeup is a masterpiece Rach will be proud of. Ky places his hand on my exposed lower back as he leads me out the door. "You look stunning, as always. I don't know what I did to deserve you."

Leaning back, I cup his head, kissing him deeply. Screw the waiting taxi driver and my friend. "You were just you, and I love you exactly as you are."

He smiles, placing me in the back of the minivan while he moves into the passenger seat. "Why are you so smug?" Rach asks, scooting over to make room for me.

"Because I'm crazy in love," I reply truthfully, not even attempting to deny it. Ky turns around, grinning at me. He lifts my hand and kisses the tips of my fingers, and I sigh dreamily. We're puke-inducing, I know that, but I couldn't care less. I'm deliriously happy, and it's the most wonderful feeling in the world. I never want to stop feeling like this.

She smacks her forehead with her palm. "God, not again. I totally understand where your cousins are coming from now. You two are disgustingly lovey-dovey, but I can't be mad at you. Not when you're so happy, because you deserve it."

"You do too." I turn to face her. She shrugs, not commenting on my statement. The taxi moves off, in the direction of Jill's house. I elbow Rach in the ribs. "So, you and Keven, huh? I want all the details. No holding back."

Ky coughs loudly. "Perhaps you can save the girl talk until I'm not in earshot."

Rach smiles. "Relax, lover boy. There's not much to tell. Your brother kissed the fuck out of me, but we didn't take it any further. I like him, and it was fun, but it's not like it's leading anywhere, so there's no need for *anyone*"—she pins me with a purposeful look—"to make a big deal out of it."

"Ouch. Way to put me in my place," I joke.

"I know you'd love me all settled and loved-up like you, and I get that it's coming from a good place, but I want different things out of life." She raises her palms. "No offense or anything."

"None taken, and that's cool. Once you're happy." We high-five as the taxi pulls up in front of Jill's house. Jill and Sam come bounding out the front door and hop in the taxi, and then we're on our way.

Club Elite is jumping when we arrive, not that I'm surprised. It isn't the most in demand hotspot for nothing. We are ushered into the VIP area and shown to our reserved table. Apparently, Kaden had called them earlier and set it up. I've never been to this club before, but I can see how it's become popular so fast. The slick interiors scream money and glamour, and it's obvious no expense has been spared. The waitress brings two buckets to our table. One contains copious bottles of beers, and the second has two large vodka bottles and accompanying mixers.

Kent stands up, rubbing his hands together. "Vodka shots coming right up!" He proceeds to fill the glasses like a pro, handing them around. Ky snakes his arm around my shoulder, rolling his eyes at his younger brother. We down a couple of shots, toasting to our trip. I spot several admiring glances leveled my cousin's way, and it's not long before our table is deluged. Girls descend like it's raining women, and pretty soon all my cousins are chatting to different girls.

Rachel is flippant as she eyes a skinny blonde in a miniscule silver mini-dress draping herself around Keven. She catches my eye. "Dance?"

Vodka buzzes through my system as I stand up, nodding. Rach tugs Jill up. "We're heading to the dance floor," I tell Ky. "You want to come?"

He shakes his head, standing to his full height. "Nah. You have fun with your friends." Reeling me into his arms, he kisses me passionately, and I melt against him. When he finally releases me, I sway a little on my heels, and he grins proudly.

Keaton stands up. "Mind if I come with?"

I loop my arm in his. "Of course not. Let's get our boogie on."

We take the stairs to the lower level and out into the middle of the heaving crowd occupying the dance floor. The air is thick with humidity as we start dancing, and I'm regretting my decision to wear the jumpsuit. Although the material is light, it's already starting to stick uncomfortably to my body. Jill and Rach had the right idea with their short, skimpy dresses. A few girls are eyeing Keaton up, but he's oblivious. I think it's sweet how loyal he is to Melissa, refusing to even lock eyes with any other girls.

After a few songs, I call a time out, desperately needing hydration. When we make our way back upstairs, the female mob surrounding our table appears to have doubled in size, and we have to fight our way through. A good-looking girl wearing the tiniest dress known to mankind is perched on the edge of the table, trying to claim Ky's attention. She crosses and uncrosses her legs, flicking her hair and wetting her lips as she angles her body toward him. He isn't giving her the time of day, chatting quietly with Sam who is also ignoring the girl trying to latch onto him from the other side. Jill's lips curl into a snarl, and I watch with amusement as she throws herself into his lap, elbowing the girl aside in the process. Ky lifts his head, and the brunette leans in to speak to him, but his attention is focused purely on me. Reaching out, he grips my waist, hauling me onto his lap and nuzzling his head in my shoulder. "These girls are fucking scary," he whispers, biting gently on my earlobe.

I crank out a laugh, but as the brunette pins me with a look Voldemort would be proud of, I can't disagree.

Rach hands me a bottle of water, not so subtly glaring at the other girl. "He's taken and you're wasting your time, so move along now."

She narrows her eyes at Rach before turning a scathing look in my direction. I can afford to be charitable, so I smile at her, curling my hands more tightly around Ky's neck as he plants a line of kisses along my jaw. Her unhappy pout speaks volumes, but she knows when she's beat. In a comical move, she slides along the table, twisting around to face Keven. Two girls are nestled on either side of him on the couch, but his hot gaze is fixated on Rach. "Excuse me, ladies." He gets up, making a beeline for my bestie, his intense gaze never wavering. Taking Rachel's hand in his, he keeps walking, holding firmly onto her. She hastily dumps her bottle on the table and lets him lead her out of the VIP room.

Ky chuckles softly against my neck as Keaton plops down on the edge of the couch, pulling at his shirt. "Haven't you guys heard of air con? It's so Goddamned hot in here."

I fan his face with my hands. "There is air conditioning." I point at the box on the far wall. "Sorry if it's not up to your exacting standards," I tease. "Ireland isn't prepared for the type of heat wave we've been experiencing."

"I'll say." He moves my hands faster, up and down, in front of his face, and I laugh.

"Here," Jill says handing him a bottle of water. "This will help you cool down."

Kent stands up on the couch, whipping his shirt up over his head. That boy is a blatant exhibitionist. A few wolf whistles ring out from the girlish posse. He winks at a couple of girls, wrapping his shirt around his naked waist. "Problem solved, bro," he hollers across the table, gesturing for Keaton to remove his shirt. Kal laughs as the girl sitting beside him drips drool out of her mouth. Keanu hops up, swaying a little as he removes his shirt too. My jaw slackens. I have never seen Keanu anything less than composed. Now, as my eyes skim over him, noting the messed-up hair and the unfocused look in his eye, I realize he's pretty smashed.

A large, older dude, wearing a black suit with shoulders the size of a bus and a fitted earpiece, approaches our table. "Gentlemen, please get down off the sofa, and put your shirts back on."

"Aw, come on, man. It's hot as fuck in here," Kent pleads with a naughty grin.

The bouncer crosses his arms. "Club rules. Put your shirts back on now."

"Dude, your rules suck," Keanu says, slurring his words a little. He slumps down on the sofa, wrestling his shirt back on.

Kaden tugs Kent down off the couch. "Don't be an ass. Just do as you're told." His look brokers no argument.

A round of protests erupts as Kent unties his shirt from his waist, reluctantly putting it back on. "Party pooper," he murmurs under his breath.

"I'm bored," Keanu suddenly announces, shucking off the amorous advances of the girl clinging to his side. "Let's hit the dance floor."

Jill hops up, dragging Sam by the arm. "I'm not taking no for an answer this time."

"I think that's our cue," Ky says, nudging Keaton out of the way.

"Thank fuck," Kal whispers in my ear, getting up to come with us. "This one is not taking the hint." He gestures at the petite blonde behind him. She's staring at him with an adoring look on her face.

"She's pretty."

"I'm not interested."

I scan my cousin's earnest face. He means it. Out of all of us, I think Kal has changed the most this last year. I hook my arm in his. "I'll protect you." I smirk.

"You'd better." He winks. "These girls are relentless."

"They know what they want, and they aren't afraid to go after it."

"I can tell, and at another time, I would've been all over what they're offering. But not anymore. There's only one girl I want, and she's not in this room."

It's the first time in months he's alluded to Lana. "I'm always here if you want to talk about it."

He gives me a quick hug. "I know. Thanks."

"How did Alex and James take the news about the University of Florida?" I ask him, as we trail the others out of the VIP room.

"They were actually pretty cool about it." He scrubs a hand over his jaw. "I expected Mom to flip out but she was fine with it."

"That's a good thing, right?"

"Totally. And they've also agreed it'd be a good idea if I was emancipated." I lift a brow. "It makes sense that I'm completely independent with the distance between us. At least this way, I can look after myself."

"And you're very sure this is what you want?" I holler in his ear as we emerge on the ground level, and the noise almost deafens me.

"One hundred percent," he shouts back.

"We'll miss you in Harvard, but I really hope it works out for you, Kal. You deserve to be happy."

His keen eyes survey me intensely, and I worry that I might have given something away. Then his shoulders relax, and I release the breath I've been holding. "Me too, and thanks."

En masse, we make our way to the dance floor with a gaggle of girls following, uninvited, in our wake.

It's crazy madness out on the floor. Throngs of dancers are jostling for space, and the heat is off the charts. Ky lines up behind me, keeping a firm arm around my waist as we dance. I spy Keven and Rach, lip-locked, in a corner of the room, and I smile to myself. The rest of my cousins are dancing, starting to mosh as they slam against one another. Swarms of girls surround them, and you'd swear there were no good-looking guys in

Dublin the way they are launching themselves at my cousins. For once, the boys seem uninterested as they deflect advances left, right, and center. Jill and I exchange amused expressions. A new, popular tune starts up, and Keanu fist pumps the air, waving his hands about excitedly, only to disappear a few seconds later. Kent is busy alternating kisses between two different girls clinging to his side. They are trading glares and insults, for obvious reasons, and it's freaking hilarious. Ky cusses under his breath, watching his younger brother like a hawk.

Kal splutters, pointing over my shoulder. He clutches his stomach, doubled over, as tears of laughter trickle down his face. Ky spins us around, and my mouth falls open. Keanu is standing up on a narrow counter at the side of the DJ booth rocking it out as the crowd roars their approval. His hands are going crazy as he dances his ass off. And, boy, can my cousin dance. He could give Justin Timberlake a run for his money any day. Keanu whips his shirt off again, this time flinging it out into the crowd, grinning like a total doofus when a few girls tussle as they reach for it.

"Ohmigawd!" Jill shrieks, laughing. "Your cousin is certifiable."

"Certifiably drunk, more like," I mumble, still struggling to believe my eyes.

"Shit," Ky exclaims, looking to the left. Two muscle-bound bouncers are advancing on the DJ booth with a ferocious look in their eye.

Chapter Six

Faye

Ky catches Kaden's eye, but he's already on it, moving in the direction of the DJ booth.

A loud roar emits from the top end of the dance floor, capturing our attention. A lone shape is running across the stage at the back of the room. My jaw slackens again as Kent launches himself off the stage into the middle of the thick crowd. I watch, aghast, as he spins through the air before landing on top of the crush of bodies surging forward to meet him. Miraculously, they manage to hold him upright, and the spike of anxiety swirling inside me retreats.

"What the actual fuck?" Ky shouts, looking at me in exasperation while shaking his head. I scan the crowd for Kent, but I've lost sight of him now his feet are back on solid ground. "He seriously needs his head examined."

"Maybe he was trying to create a distraction?" I suggest.

Ky scoffs. "He didn't like the fact Keanu was getting all the attention, so he did something to draw it back on himself. Honestly, I worry about his mental stability a lot."

"He's not the only one you should worry about." I nudge his shoulder, pointing toward the DJ box. Keanu is being dragged off the counter by one of the bouncers, and his expression is sheepish as he peers at the floor. The bouncer twists his hands behind his back, holding them in a vise-grip, while Kaden argues animatedly with the other bouncer.

"That was frigging awesome, dude!" Kent exclaims, rejoining us, with an ecstatic smile on his face.

"That was frigging idiotic," Ky retorts, his nostrils flaring as he swats the back of Kent's head. "You could've seriously injured yourself."

"Quit with the bitching, *Dad*. You're so boring these days."

"I thought it was brilliant," the slutty blonde with the smudged mascara says. The other girl seems to have given up and disappeared. "And I think you deserve a reward." Stretching up, she grabs his face in both her tiny hands and smashes her lips against his. Kent pulls her in flush to his body, grinding his hips against hers in a deliberate move.

Ky moves forward, but I hold him back. "Don't get involved. It's not worth it." It isn't. It won't make a blind bit of difference, and all it will do is cause another argument.

Rach appears in my line of sight. Keven has her tucked possessively under his arm as he stalks through the crowd toward us. "What's going on?" he asks Ky, keeping a tight hold on Rach.

"Just the usual crap." Ky glances over his shoulder and cusses. "Great. They're kicking Keanu out." We all turn around. The same bouncer is now hauling Keanu toward the exit. Kaden eyeballs us, and Ky nods. "Time to go."

I spin around, smothering a grin as Kent's grabby hands slip under the hem of blondie's dress. "Good luck getting him out of here."

Kev and Ky share a loaded look. "You get the others out safely, and I'll handle the little shit," Ky tells his older brother. Kev nods and starts rounding up the others. Ky sighs, scrubbing a hand over his stubbly jaw. "This is not how I saw this night going."

"Never a dull moment," I joke, trying to cut a line through the strain.

Ky takes a step forward, but a hulk of a guy shoves him out of the way as he barrels toward Kent. Ky stumbles and I reach out, grabbing his arm to keep him upright. "What the heck? Are you okay?" I peer into his face.

"Oh shit!" Ky's jaw clenches as he stares over my shoulder. I spin around just as the hulk reaches Kent and the blonde-haired girl. Roughly yanking her away, he pushes her to one side. Another guy steps forward, wrapping an arm around the girl's waist. She doesn't even attempt to protest, slumping in his arms with a frightened look on her face.

Kent's chin juts up as he attempts to outstare the other guy. "What the fuck is your problem, bro?"

"My problem, bro," the guy says, in a thick inner-city Dublin accent, "is your hands were all over my woman, and no one touches my Zara. No one."

A group of rough-looking guys force their way through the crowd, heading in our direction. All the tiny hairs lift on my arms. Ky turns to me. "Shit's about to get real, and I want you nowhere near this. Go get Kev and Kade for me, and then stay outside with the others." I open my mouth to protest, but he plants a quick, hot kiss on my lips. "No time to argue. Please. Just do as I say."

Reluctantly, I nod and take off running. I catch up to Rach and Kev at the edge of the dance floor and quickly explain. Kev utters a volley of colorful expletives. "Go outside and get Kade. Then you two stay out there. This could get messy," he commands, before disappearing onto the dance floor.

I make a split-second decision. "I'm going back. They might need a local to help defuse things. Can you explain everything to Kaden and tell him to hurry?"

She nods quickly. "'Kay. Be careful."

"I will."

I shove my way forcefully through the crowd, my anxiety rising a few notches the deeper I get. A small circle has formed in the area where I last left Ky and my cousins, and I can see jack shit. Bile rises up my throat. I have a really bad feeling about this. Those guys are the type you don't mess around with. Kent may think he's all badass, but he's no match for the likes of those boys. They won't hesitate to beat his ass until he can barely breathe.

I frantically search the perimeters of the room. *Where the fuck are the bouncers when you need them?*

I elbow my way through the nosy mob blocking my path, ignoring the obscenities flung my way. Little beads of sweat dot my brow, and a line coasts down the gap between my breasts. I swallow the panic in my throat as the sounds of fighting reach my ears. Girls start fleeing, screaming as they run off the dance floor. More guys descend from out of nowhere, jumping into the fray. I blink profusely as I grapple with the images in front of me. At least twenty guys are brawling in the middle of the dance floor, and my boyfriend and two of my cousins are in the thick of it.

The hulk is raining blows on Kent, and Kent's thrashing about, swinging his arms wildly. The hulk is a beast of a guy, but he's remarkably nimble on his feet, effortlessly avoiding all of Kent's punches. Kent isn't so fortunate. I wince as the guy rams his fist in Kent's face, and his head jerks back.

Terror and anger are an explosive mix inside me, and my brain shuts off. I'm blaming my slightly inebriated state for what I do next. Blood spurts out of Kent's nose as the hulk moves in again. Racing toward them, I fling myself on the hulk's back, jumping up and wrapping my legs around his waist as I haul myself up his body. I circle my arm around his meaty neck and tighten it, yanking as hard as I can, while cementing my grip on his torso with my legs. You could spray paint me on his body, and I wouldn't be welded as tightly to him.

"Da fuck?" the guy fumes, moving back and forth in an attempt to throw me off.

I cling on harder. "Get the fuck away from my cousin. It's not his fault your girlfriend is a cheating little slut. She was all over him, not the other way around." It's no word of a lie. Those girls pursued him; he didn't go looking for them.

Reaching up, the hulk grabs my arm and squeezes, hard. A dart of pain zips up my arm, and I cry out. "Get off me, bitch," he snarls.

Kent is struggling to his feet. "Don't you fucking touch her, asshole," he screams, spitting blood as he stalks toward us.

Strong hands grip my waist and tug. Caught off guard by the unexpected move, I automatically loosen my hold on the hulk, and he reacts fast, tipping me back with force. The arms at my back let go, and I scream as I feel myself falling. In desperation, I grab onto the hulk's neck, digging my nails into his flesh as I fight the falling sensation. With a guttural roar, he swings around, throwing me off him with force. I soar through the air like a bird. Closing my eyes, I offer up a prayer as I prepare myself for a crash landing. Someone kills the music, and screams and shouts reverberate around the club as I sail toward the floor. I land on someone, my head slamming against a hard chest. A familiar groan has my eyes popping wide, and I twist around. Ky is underneath me, moaning as his arms fasten around my waist.

"Oh my God! Are you all right?" I cup his face. "Babe, are you okay?"

"I think you broke me," he rasps in a choked voice.

"Oh God. Where does it hurt?" Panic undercuts my tone at the thought that he might have broken his back or a leg or something.

"My dick," he splutters, as I'm scrambling off him.

"What?" I screech. "This is hardly the time for cracking jokes." I scan the half-empty dance floor. A larger crowd is kicking the shit out of one another in the center of the floor while everyone else is running for the hills. I can't see Keven or Kent in the writhing mass of bodies. Punches are flying in all directions as a member of staff urges everyone—over the loudspeaker—to evacuate the club.

I stagger to my bare feet, wondering where the hell my shoes are. Thankfully, I have my emergency fold-up ballet flats in my bag.

Ky tries to sit up, cupping his groin. "You elbowed me in the balls when I caught you," he explains, answering my silent question. "Fuuuuccckkk!" He squeezes his eyes shut, wincing in pain.

Up ahead, a group of six bouncers is attempting to break up the fight. A thinner, older guy with cropped gray hair stands off to one side talking urgently into a mouthpiece. He shakes his head at the bouncers, and, as one, they fall back, watching events from the safety of the sideline.

That can only mean one thing.

"We have to get out of here now, Ky. They've called the police."

"Help me up." He extends an arm, and I pull him to his feet. He is bent over, still cradling his crotch, and huge guilt waylays me.

"Sorry. I should've listened to you."

"Let's just focus on getting out of here without anyone getting arrested."

Someone shouts my name, and I whirl around. Kev has a hold of Kent's arm, and he's dragging him away from the fighting. Both of them are bloody and cut up, but they don't appear to have sustained any serious injuries.

Kal and Kade appear in front of us. "I hear police sirens in the distance. We need to get the hell out of here," Kade says, cursing when he spies the state of his brothers.

"Take Faye's hand," Ky says through gritted teeth, eyeballing Kal. "And don't let go. Get her out of here now."

"What the fuck, man?" Kal asks, frowning as he grips my hand.

"Elbow in the balls," Ky whimpers, hobbling after us.

"Ouch." Kal's face scrunches into a painful grimace, and I roll my eyes. *Seriously? How painful can it really be? It's not like it's bloody childbirth.* Wisely, I keep those thoughts to myself as we flee the club.

Outside, Keaton is crouched over Keanu as he pukes up his guts in the alleyway alongside the club. Sam has one arm around Rach and one arm around Jill. He straightens up as he spots us. "I know a shortcut. Follow me." The blaring noise of the sirens draws nearer, and he glances briefly over his shoulder. "But let's make it snappy." Keaton helps Keanu up, and we all run down the alley after Sam.

I have a stitch in my side, and my feet are sore, but I say nothing, fueled by adrenaline and a potent desire not to become acquainted with the inside of a garda station. After about fifteen minutes, we emerge onto a quieter, less well-known street, and Sam slows his pace until we come to a halt. Everyone is gasping for breath and taking a moment to let recent events sink in.

"Holy shit," Keaton exclaims, being the first to break the silence. "That was some fucked-up shit back there."

A loud snort of laughter erupts from somewhere inside me. I collapse onto the pavement, clutching my stomach as I bust out laughing. Relief washes over me, as I contemplate how disastrous that could've been. One by one, everyone joins in, and it helps to ease the tense atmosphere.

"Shit, those Dublin dudes are not to be messed with," Kent begrudgingly admits.

"I'm glad you've learned that lesson early in the vacation," Kade deadpans. "I did not come on this trip to be your babysitter."

"Nor me," Ky pipes up, sounding more like himself now. He's stopped cupping his groin, so I figure that mini-drama is over.

"I didn't ask either of you to babysit me," Kent grumbles. "I'm more than capable of looking after myself."

"Stop talking shit, Kent," Kev speaks up, glaring at his younger brother. "You could be dead right now if we hadn't waded in to save your ass."

"Your brother is right," Rach adds. "You don't want to get mixed up with those fuckers."

Kent mumbles something incoherent under his breath, but we all ignore him.

"What now?" Jill asks.

Ky looks at his watch. "It's late. Time to call it a night, I think."

"We need to get them cleaned up," I supply, motioning at Kent and Keven. "We can't send them back to the hotel looking like that. Your mom will throw a hissy fit."

"I've got a first aid kit at home. Why don't you swing by my house, and we can patch the guys up there?" Rach suggests.

Her house is closer than mine so it makes the most sense. "Sounds like a plan." I get up, brushing bits of dust and debris off my now very filthy jumpsuit.

Jill summons a couple of Halos on her phone, while Ky wraps his arms around me from behind, nestling his chin on my shoulder. "You okay now?" I ask, tilting my head around to look at him.

"Yeah. No permanent damage." He smirks.

"Yeah, um, sorry about that."

His smirk turns to a scowl. "Thought I told you to stay out of the fray?"

"I thought you might need a local to help talk your way out of the situation. I didn't realize it had already turned into fisticuffs at dawn. Then I saw that knucklehead beating on Kent and I got mad."

"So that's why you decided to jump on his back like a spider monkey?"

I shrug. "Seemed like a good idea at the time."

He shakes his head, but he doesn't seem too mad at me. "What am I going to do with you?"

"I can think of plenty of things," I reply saucily, and a flare of desire sparks in his eyes.

"That reminds me. Someone owes me a rain check," he whispers, and his hot breath on my ear does funny things to my insides.

I fight a smile. "And that someone is happy to oblige once we get home."

Jill and Sam take one taxi with Kade and Kal while the rest of us take an eight-seater to Rach's house.

Once inside, she retrieves the first aid kit, opening it up on the marble countertop in the kitchen. Ky is currently in the living room, plying Keanu with water and coffee in an attempt to sober him up. Keaton is sprawled lengthways on the leather sofa, snoring his head off.

Keven and Kent are seated on stools in the kitchen while Rach and I attend to their injuries. I don't miss the myriad of looks being exchanged between my cousin and my friend, and it wouldn't surprise me if Kev didn't return to the hotel tonight.

"This might sting," I warn Kent, dabbing a cotton pad in some warm water and pressing it to his nose. He flinches, grinding down on his molars as I gently clean all the blood away. He has a few contusions to his jaw and his left cheek, and his nose is already swollen and discolored, but nothing is broken or requires professional medical treatment. "You'll need to come up with one hell of an excuse to explain all the bruises to your parents."

"I'll just tell them the truth," he says, surprising me. "Not like they can do anything about it."

My eyes flit to his, while rubbing some arnica cream into his cheek. "Why do you do this all the time?" I'm expecting some smartass response, but he just shrugs. I finish cleaning him up in silence.

Rach and Kev are quietly kissing as I round up all the wet cloths and bloody tissues and take them to the bin. Kent jumps down from the stool, shoving his hands in his pockets and shuffling awkwardly on his feet. "Thanks."

"No problem." I smile.

"And thanks for tonight. I appreciate what you tried to do."

Well, knock me down with a feather. Kent is actually being serious for a change. And showing gratitude. Wonders will never cease. "I was hardly going to stand around and watch some asshole beat on my cousin and do nothing about it." I gulp over the sudden lump of emotion in my throat. "Family means everything to me, Kent. I care about all of you so much."

A terrified expression flares in his eyes. "Please don't cry or get all gushy and emotional. I can't handle that shit."

And just like that, the Kent I'm more familiar with is back. I grin, mussing up his hair. "Don't worry. I think you've had enough shit for one night."

"Thank fuck." He winks, sauntering past me out to the living room.

Subtle moans and groans echo in the quiet kitchen, and I clear my throat. "Ahem."

Rach reluctantly pulls away from Keven, running her tongue over her swollen lips. "This better be good, girlfriend."

I laugh. "We're going to head now." I drill a piercing look at my cousin. "Are you coming with us or staying here?"

He looks up at Rach, and some unspoken communication filters between them. Kev pulls my bestie onto his lap, eyeballing me over her shoulder. "I'm staying here."

"Grand." I lean in and hug my friend. "I'll text you tomorrow."

I rally the others, and, between Ky and me, we manage to get a hungover Keanu, injured Kent, and sleeping Keaton into the Halo in one piece. We drop them off at the hotel before heading back to my house.

When we eventually flop into bed, it's well after four a.m. Ky is snoring the instant his head hits the pillow, and I chuckle. So much for rain checks.

Chapter Seven

Kyler

Faye makes good on her rain check the next morning, and I drive us to the hotel in plenty of time to meet the family for breakfast. Mom takes one look at Kent's face and explodes. Dad just shakes his head in exasperation. Kade is still tucked up in bed, and he's refusing to join us. Kev is a no-show so far, but Mom doesn't look displeased at the news he stayed at Rachel's last night. I think she likes Faye's best friend, and she probably wouldn't mind if something were to happen between them.

Not that it will. There's the little matter of the Atlantic Ocean separating them and the fact that neither of them are into relationships. The last girlfriend Keven had was in high school. When he broke up with Cheryl their senior year, he was devastated, and I don't think he's ever gotten over her. I don't know what went down between them, but it was a damn shame they didn't last the distance. She was a real sweetheart and perfect for Kev in so many ways.

Come to think of it, all his troubles only started after that time.

Faye's hand lands on my thigh under the table. "Hey. You okay?"

I press a kiss to her forehead. "I'm perfect. Just thinking about stuff."

"Should I be worried?"

I smooth the furrow in her brow with my thumb. "Nope. I'm good."

She relaxes, squeezing my thigh playfully. "I'm going to go to the graveyard with your dad in a few minutes. Kal and Keaton are coming too, but I think you should stay to keep your mom company. I know she missed you like crazy."

I sweep her hair back off her forehead, conscious of Mom slyly watching us. "You sure?"

"Positive." She leans in to my ear. "Maybe you can get the lowdown on her and your dad?"

I roll my eyes. Faye has her heart set on the two of them reuniting. If I'm honest, I'm rooting for them too. We all are. But none of us want to get our hopes up either. While Mom and Dad haven't divorced yet, they've lived separately for eight months now. The longer they are apart, the less likely reconciliation seems.

"Who's playing matchmaker now?" I tease.

Her eyes sparkle. "I'm an eternal optimist," she declares with a wink. "And they seem to be getting on well so far."

"That's one of the things I love about you." I press a soft kiss to her mouth, uncaring that my mother is still watching. "And you're right. They are."

"Are you coming with us or staying here, Kyler?" Dad asks, rising from his seat.

"I think I'll pass. I visited with Faye last week."

He slaps me on the back. "You can keep your mother company then, and round up your wayward brothers."

After Dad, Faye, and my brothers leave, Mom orders more coffee and pastries as we wait for Kade and Kev to grace us with their presence. Kent and Keanu have gone for a swim in the hotel pool. "Things seem to be getting very serious with Faye," she says, licking the froth off the back of her spoon.

I level her with a look. "Things have always been serious with Faye."

Her responding smile is warm. "Should I prepare myself for an official announcement?"

I nearly spit my coffee out on the table. "Relax, Mom. We're only eighteen."

She flaps her hands in the air. "Age is only a number when it comes to love."

I sit back, crossing one leg over the other. "I don't disagree, but I'm in no rush to race Faye to the altar. It's going to happen, and I'll do it when the timing feels right."

"I'm very proud of you, Kyler."

My brow puckers. "Okay?" My tone carries my confusion.

She laughs softly, and she looks so young and carefree in the moment. "You've gone through a lot in the last year, but you've come out of it stronger than before. I'm proud of the way you've handled yourself and so thankful that you found it in your heart to forgive me."

I reach over the table, taking her hands in mine. "I've come to terms with all that, and you're my mother. I, ah"—I squirm uncomfortably in my seat—"I love you, Mom, and I know you've always tried your best to do right by us."

She slides out of her seat, crossing to my side, and slips in the booth beside me. Her arms envelop me in a giant hug. "I love you too, son. So much." Her voice cracks and her eyes are shiny, and I wonder how the fuck we ended up having this conversation. I know Faye has brought my softer side to the fore, but I'm still not used to airing my feelings so freely in front of either of my parents.

She cups my face, pressing a gentle kiss to my cheek. "And I love Faye as if she already is my daughter. I think you know that, but I wanted to say it aloud. You two are perfect for each other, and it warms my heart to see you both so happy and in love." A nostalgic look glistens in her eye. "It reminds me of when I met James. The way you look at Faye is the way he used to look at me." She smiles sadly, folding her hands in her lap.

I clear my throat. "Do you think there's any possibility you and Dad might get back together?"

"I don't know." Nervously, she tucks strands of her blonde hair behind her ears. "I will always love him, but I hurt him a lot too, and I don't know if that's ever something he can get over."

"But he hurt you too."

She nods. "Yes, he did, but, as the saying goes, two wrongs don't make a right."

Silence engulfs us.

"How come you haven't divorced yet?" I ask after a bit.

"I don't think either of us are in a rush to do that," she admits quietly. "But if your father wanted that, I wouldn't stand in his way."

"Have you spoken to him about it?"

"Not really, and I don't want to rock the boat. Things are good the way they are, and unless he feels otherwise, or if the time comes when I feel differently, I'm happy to leave things for now."

"Do you want me to talk to Dad?" I offer, twisting around to face her head-on.

She cups my face again. "No, sweetheart. I understand you want to help, but you have to let us deal with things on our own."

I swallow the wedge of emotion in my throat. "Sure."

An awkward throat clearing has me looking up. Kev has his arms folded across his chest, his gaze flipping from me to Mom. "Am I interrupting?" His brows nudge up.

"Not at all, sweetheart." Mom jumps up, encasing him in a mammoth hug. "Sit down and I'll order you some breakfast unless Rachel already took care of that?" Her teasing tone matches her grin.

"She was still sleeping when I left," he sheepishly admits.

Mom lightly slaps his arm, frowning a little. "That's not very nice, Keven. I thought I'd raised you better than that."

Kev groans, dropping into the booth across from us. "Mom, don't."

Mom scowls, and Kev stares up at the ceiling. I fail to keep the smirk off my face as I settle back in my seat, glad the heat is directed at someone else for a change.

"Rachel's a lovely girl, and she deserves to be treated with respect." Mom isn't going to let this go anytime soon.

Kev leans over the table. "I agree, Mom, but I didn't want to wake her when she looked so peaceful. I also didn't want to be late for today's excursion, so that's why I left a note on her pillow explaining everything." Kev looks like he's just swallowed something sour, and I laugh at his uncomfortable expression. It's killed him to admit something so sweet.

Mom's eyes glisten mischievously, and I get the sense she's totally playing with him. "I approve, darling." She pats his hand. "Of the girl and the gesture."

Kev smacks his palm against his forehead, groaning. "Mom, just stop. Please. Nothing is going to happen, okay. We're just having a bit of fun while I'm here so don't go reading into things."

Mom holds up her hands. "Okay, okay. I'll say no more." She shoots me a grin, and I grin back as Kade appears at the table, tapping away on his phone.

He plonks down alongside Kev without even looking up. Mom rolls her eyes. "Kaden."

"Just a sec, Mom," he says, without altering his focus.

Kev's eyes narrow as he slants a brooding stare at Kade. Kade's lips twitch as he texts, and I share a loaded look with my other brother. Mom summons the waiter, ordering more food and coffee. Kade finally looks up, slipping his cell into his pocket and propping his elbows on the table. "Where is everyone?" he asks the same time Kev speaks up.

"Who were you texting?"

"None of your business," Kade instantly replies, sending Kev a "drop it" look.

My curiosity is immediately piqued. "Please tell me it wasn't that Tiffani chick."

"What if it was?" Kade's expression is challenging.

"Then your taste is in the toilet, dude."

His lips curve up at the corner. "That's not very nice, Kyler. Tiffani happens to be a sweet girl."

Mom frowns a little. "I'm not denying that, but she doesn't seem right for you."

Kade leans back in his seat, stretching his arm out along the back of the booth. His brows kick up. "Since when has my family become experts in who is or isn't right for me?"

The conversation is momentarily halted when the waiter arrives with breakfast for my brothers.

"Why do you have to be so secretive?" Kev asks, cutting into his bacon with more vigor than necessary.

Kade's fork clangs to the table as he pins an incredulous look at him. "Three words. Pot. Kettle. Black." He lifts his fork, jabbing it at Keven as his amused attitude turns sour. "Butt out of stuff that doesn't concern you."

"Screw you," Kev retorts, glaring at him. I sit more upright in my seat. Kev has hinted at issues with Kade previously, but I didn't realize things were so acrimonious between them, and I can't help wondering how it got to this point. My older brothers have always been tight, in a way that used to make me feel jealous. Looking at it now, I can't figure out where things went wrong or why.

"Please don't argue, boys. I want this trip to be argument free," Mom beseeches.

I snort. Sorry, can't help it. "Then you should have gone away with a different family."

♥♥♥♥♥♥♥

A couple of hours later, once everyone has returned and we are all ready, we set out for another action-packed day full of tourist crap. I seriously don't know how I get through the day without murdering Kent. He never stops grumbling and moaning the entire time. I get it. Mom is dragging us around places we have zero interest in, but this is important to her, and I don't mind indulging her. I can't remember the last time we were all on vacation together, and it could be the last time we get to do this, so I shut my mouth and go with the flow.

We grab a quick dinner in the hotel before heading to Croke Park for the highlight of Dad and Kal's trip: a U2 gig. Croke Park is one of Dublin's key sporting and concert venues, according to Faye and the brochures Mom picked up on the way in, and it's only fitting that the legends of Irish rock are performing here. I don't share my dad's and my younger brother's U2 obsession, but I don't mind their stuff either. Watching Dad and Kal in matching U2 shirts shoving their way through the enthusiastic crowd to the front of the stage is pure gold. Sometimes, I think my dad forgets he's turning forty this year. I hang back with Mom, Faye, and Kaden, content to hold my baby in my arms as we sway to the music.

Tuesday is another day of adventure in Dublin, with Mom lugging us all over the city in a rush to pack as much as possible into our last day. That night, after an interesting dinner in a Korean fusion restaurant that offers a buffet-style BBQ, and comes complete with guests belly-dancing on the tables and my brothers competing in a sing-off in one of the karaoke rooms upstairs, Faye and I return to her house for the last time.

Tomorrow, we are traveling to Cork, and over the weekend, we are meeting up with Faye's father, Adam, in Wexford.

After we have packed up our stuff, we retreat to the sitting room with a bottle of wine. We snuggle on the sofa as we watch some detective show on Netflix. "You sad to be leaving?" I ask, threading my fingers through her hair.

"A bit."

"That's understandable."

"I've enjoyed spending time here more than I thought I would," she admits, twisting around so she's looking into my face.

I tighten my arm around her waist, pressing a kiss to her forehead. "I'm glad. Have you made any decisions yet about the house?"

She slowly nods. "I don't want to sell it. Mum loved this house, and I see her touch everywhere I look. If I was still living in Ireland, I don't know if I could bear to live here and be reminded of my loss every day. But having it as a place to retreat to in the summer and on other holidays actually appeals to me."

"Me too." I purse my lips. "Assuming the invitation extends to me?"

She pinches my arm. "Asshole." I chuckle. "As if I'd ever be going anywhere without you."

Chapter Eight

Faye

James has hired a chauffeur-driven minibus to take us down the country, and we set off early on Wednesday morning for Cork. Closing the door to my family home is sad but not as traumatic as the last time I pulled the door shut on this aspect of my life. Last year—when James showed up—I had no idea where I was going, what I was getting myself into, or when, or if, I might be back. Things are more settled now, and I know I'll be returning so my heart isn't as heavy this time.

Traveling to Cork on a luxury minibus with my rambunctious cousins reminds me of that movie *National Lampoon's Vacation*. Mum made me watch it one time, and I found myself roaring with laughter despite the cheesiness. As I surreptitiously scan the bus, watching my cousins arguing and laughing, shoving and pushing one another, a surge of happiness washes over me. Unconsciously, I nestle in closer to Ky's side, intertwining our hands.

"You okay, babe?" he asks in a sleepy voice.

His seat is reclined and he's been dozing for the last hour while I've been reading. "I'm perfect." I wrap my arm around his waist. "I love you." Sometimes, I just feel an overwhelming urge to tell him. It can be at the most random of times, but I don't ignore the instinct. On countless occasions, I've wondered if I told my parents enough that I loved them. If they died knowing how much they meant to me. From now on, I'm not going to shy away from telling the people I love how

I feel about them. My thoughts wander to Adam—my bio dad—as they have a lot these last few weeks. I have yet to utter those words to him. Not out of any fear of saying them, more so that it's taken me some time to decipher my feelings. I also firmly believe that love shouldn't be flippantly traded. It's too easy for some people to throw out an "I love you." When I say it, I mean it, with the totality of what's in my heart.

"Love you too," Ky mumbles, curling into me.

"Pass me the puke bucket," Kent protests from the row across. "I just threw up in my mouth."

I flip him the bird. "You need some new insults, Kent. It's starting to get old."

"I wish your love would. Then we wouldn't have to suffer so much."

Keaton elbows him sharply in the ribs. "Don't be mean, and you know that's never going to happen." He winks at me, and I blow him a kiss.

"You're right, Keats. My love for Ky will never die." I burst out laughing. "Ha! That even rhymes." I'm rather proud of my cheesiness.

"Fuck. Someone help me, please." Kent slams his palm into his forehead. "Or shoot me, or something."

I snort. "At the rate you're clocking up enemies, I'm sure that can easily be arranged."

Kent elbows Keaton in the ribs.

"Ow!" Keaton cries. "What was that for?"

"So, it's okay for her to speak to me like that?" He pouts, and I can barely contain my laughter. Kent never fails to entertain me.

"What are you, like, five again?" Keaton shakes his head in frustration.

Kent pouts again, pulling his headphones on. "Whatever. I'm bored with this conversation."

I share a smile with Keaton as I get out of my seat, carefully tiptoeing around Ky so as not to wake him now that he's dozing again. "Where you going?" he whispers.

"To speak to your dad."

I move up a few rows, plonking myself down in the empty seat beside James. He marks the page in his book and closes it, smiling at me. "Hey, sweetheart." He presses a kiss to the top of my head.

"Do you have a minute?"

He beams at me. "For my favorite niece? Always."

I mock scowl. "I'm your *only* niece."

"You're still my favorite."

I shake my head, fighting a smile. "You're my favorite uncle too."

He throws back his head and laughs. "I know when I'm beat. What's up?"

"I wanted to talk to you about the house."

His expression turns serious. "I'm all ears."

"I'm going to hold onto it. It doesn't feel right to sell it." He nods. "But I'm going to need to find someone, a housekeeper-type person, to keep an eye on it. To make sure it's clean and that the grass is cut, etcetera, but I don't have the first idea how to go about finding such a person, and I was wondering if you could help?"

"Of course. Leave that to me and Alex. We'll deal with it."

"Thank you. That would be a weight off my mind."

"No problem. Happy to help."

We are quiet for a couple of minutes, but it's not awkward. "Can I ask you something? If it's too personal, you can tell me to butt out."

He arches a brow. "Go on."

I wet my lips, wondering if Ky will be mad that I'm about to cross a line. I know he doesn't want me to play matchmaker, but I haven't missed the little looks and touches that James and Alex have been sharing on this trip, and my gut tells me they still have strong feelings for one other. Maybe I'm trapped in a rose-tinted love bubble, because I'm so deliriously in love, or maybe it's another consequence of my parents passing before their time, but it doesn't feel right not to say something when two people obviously still care about each other a lot. "You and Alex seem to be getting on really well on the trip, and I know you guys haven't divorced, and I think you both still care about each other, and I was just wondering if you might be getting back together?" My word vomit comes to an abrupt halt.

His chest heaves, and he looks absently out the window. I chew on the inside of my mouth, wondering if I should take it back. If I've inadvertently hurt him. He turns to me, smiling a little as he takes my hands in his. "It's sweet of you to think of us, and, yes, we are getting on well, but it's a lot more complicated than that."

"Oh." My face drops. "I'm sorry if that was rude. It's just I know my cousins are secretly hoping you're going to get back together, and it's so sad you aren't with each other anymore."

He sighs. "I had a feeling they felt like that, but none of them have come outright and admitted it. You know how boys are." He chuckles. "All I can say is things are good between Alex and I, and for the first time in ages, we can be in each other's company without hurting one another or constantly arguing. I don't know if it will ever be more than that but, for now, I'm happy with where we've landed and I've no desire to change that."

"Not that it makes any difference or anything, but I'm rooting for you guys."

James smiles. "Ah, I see. Well, thank you, honey. That's very sweet of you."

My cheeks flare up, and I wonder what on earth possessed me to strike up such a conversation. I hop up. "I'm going to check on Ky. Make sure he's okay," I mutter, my embarrassment escalating as I hightail it out of there with my uncle grinning at my discomfort.

♥♥♥♥♥♥♥

We arrive in Cork at lunchtime and check into our five-star hotel. The next day and a half passes by in a blur as we visit all the major tourist sights on Alex's exhaustive list. Early on Friday morning, we hop back on the bus and take the two-hour trip to Kerry, stopping to take pictures of the incredible scenery along the route. Alex drags us to a couple of tourist sights, and we arrive in Killarney as daylight is fading, checking into another plush hotel.

The receptionist recommends an Italian restaurant in the town for dinner, and after we've stuffed our faces, we move to a bar a few doors down, somehow managing to find a table in the packed room just as a traditional music session starts up. James taps his knee up and down, happily guzzling his pint of Guinness. Alex hums and sways to the music, smiling like she hasn't a care in the world. The woman she is today is a world away from that stressed, overwrought businesswoman I first met. I rest my head on Ky's shoulder as I sip my vodka, watching his parents chat and laugh easily. I know what my uncle said to me earlier in the week, and I can't decide if he's in denial or he just didn't want to admit his feelings to his niece. But there is nothing anyone can say to make me believe those two aren't falling in love all over again.

"Your parents look happy," I whisper in Ky's ear.

"I noticed too." His smile is optimistic. "This trip was the best idea ever. I don't know why we didn't do more of this."

"Because your mom was always working."

"True." He takes a swig from his bottle of beer. "But she could have made time."

"I'm sure she has plenty of regrets." I stand up. "I need the bathroom." Bending down, I peck his lips. "Be back in a sec."

Maneuvering a path to the ladies requires considerable skill, but I navigate the crammed bar like a pro. The locals are all really friendly, greeting me as if I'm a long-lost friend. Mum would've loved it here.

I step out into the corridor leading to the bathrooms, greedily gulping in the cooler air. It's roasting in the bar, and tendrils of sweat roll down my spine.

Keanu is up ahead, with his back facing me, leaning into the wall outside the gents as he huddles over his phone. "Take deep breaths, Selena. It's okay. You've got this." My sneakers are soft as I walk toward him. "I know. I know. I'm sorry. But it won't be too much longer. I'll be home in a little over a week." He straightens up as he senses me approaching. His head whips around, and he eyeballs me. "I've got to go. I'll call you back later." I stop, lounging against the opposite wall. "I promise." He looks down at the floor as he mumbles, "Love you, too."

Aw, it's so cute, but I work really hard to keep a straight face knowing Keanu wouldn't appreciate the sentiment.

He pockets his phone and lifts his head up. "Faye."

"Hey. I didn't mean to earwig, but is Selena okay?"

He bites his lower lip as he considers my question. "She's on her first shoot without me, and she's a little nervous. She just wanted to hear my voice."

I'm surprised he admitted that. Keanu is notoriously mute when it comes to his girlfriend. Even his brothers know next to nothing about

Selena, and she's never been over at the house. Not even once, which I find really weird. Ky and I bumped into them last year when we were in Boston that time my friends visited, but that's the only time I've met her, and it was fleeting. "She's never modeled with anyone else?" The incredulity in my tone is transparent. Not that I'm any expert on the modeling industry, but that seems odd.

"Her only modeling gig was Kennedy Apparel, and she only ever modeled on her own or with me. However, she's no choice but to be more flexible now that Accardi owns the label, and they are less understanding than Mom was. They had to line up a replacement male model for the shoot today, considering I'm out of the country, and Selena's a little freaked."

Worry lines dot his brow, and I can tell he's genuinely concerned. "Try not to worry. I'm sure she'll be fine, and there are others on the shoot, right? It's not like she'll be alone with the guy?"

His eyes assess me astutely, but I'm not sure why. "No, she won't. And she'll be fine. You're right." He smiles but it looks forced. "I better get back before Mom sends out a search party," he jokes, but I'm not buying it. There's something off about Keanu's relationship that I can't put my finger on.

"Sure. I'll see you back there in a bit," I say, pushing my curiosity aside. Perhaps Ky is right. Other people's relationships are none of my business, even if they're family and I care about them. It doesn't give me the right to stick my nose where it's clearly not wanted. And from the vibes Keanu's emitting, I can tell that's exactly the case.

Chapter Nine

Kyler

I'm watching Faye battle her way back to our table when a loud jolt has me jumping in my seat. "What the actual fuck?" Kade roars. Rage simmers behind his eyes as he glares at Kev.

"Kaden. Watch your language, and keep your voice down!" Mom hisses, her cheeks staining with embarrassment as she quickly looks around.

Kaden ignores her, continuing to glare at Kev as they maintain a silent face off. Veins protrude in Kade's neck, and he clenches and unclenches his fists at his side. When he speaks, it's through gritted teeth. "Just because you *can* invade someone's privacy doesn't mean you should do it."

Oh, fuck. *What the hell did Kev do?*

Faye slides on to the stool beside me, her gaze bouncing between my brothers. "What's going on?" she whispers. "What did I miss?"

I lean in, pressing my mouth close to her ear. "I don't really know, but shit's about to hit the fan." Both my older brothers are stubborn as fuck, and from their stiff postures and glacial expressions, I can tell neither of them is ready to step down.

"Sometimes *someone* doesn't know what's best for them and it's necessary to intervene," Kev retorts in a carefully controlled voice.

Kade slams his fist down hard, shaking the table and rattling all the glasses. Mom is about to blow a gasket.

"Whatever this is," Dad hurriedly cuts in, "you can take it outside before you embarrass your mother any further." A quick look over my shoulder confirms we're starting to draw unwelcome attention.

Kade stands, stalking toward the front entrance without saying a word. Steam is practically billowing out of his ears. Kev gets up to follow, and I jump up, applying light pressure to his arm as I hold onto him. "You want me to come with?"

He shakes my hand off. "Leave it, Ky. This doesn't involve you."

I'm seething when I sit back down, and a muscle pulses in my jaw.

"He didn't mean anything by that," Faye murmurs in a soothing voice.

I rub the back of my stiff neck. "Yes, he did. This is exactly how those two get. They are always so damned secretive, and they always keep shit from me."

She takes my hand, linking her fingers in mine. "Things will be different come September. Once we are all in Harvard, I bet they'll open up to you more."

I harrumph. "I don't care," I lie, but hurt radiates from my words.

Wordlessly, she wraps her arms around my waist, cuddling into my side. Some of my anger and hurt ebbs away. A heavy layer of tension has settled on our table though, obliterating the previous chill vibes, and I could kill my brothers for spoiling the mood. The band continues to entertain the crowd, and we listen quietly, all conversation halted as everyone is locked in their own thoughts. A few minutes pass, and then I feel a hand on my back. A tall guy with slim shoulders and reddish-brown hair leans over me. "Are those your brothers out front?" His lyrical Irish accent is pronounced. I nod sharply. "Then I think you need to get out there," he says ominously before walking away.

I get up. Everyone is staring at me expectantly. I shrug. "I'm going outside to check. Stay here." Faye stands up, lacing her fingers in mine and jutting her chin out defiantly. I don't even bother arguing with her. Keeping her close to my back, I maintain a hold of her hand, as I navigate a path out of the bar.

"Ho. Lee. Shit," Faye exclaims, clamping a hand over her mouth as we step out on the sidewalk. Darkness has encroached on the nighttime sky, but my brothers are well lit under the full glare of the streetlights.

Kade's head jerks back as Kev lands a solid punch to his jaw. Kade staggers a little, recovering quickly and launching a fast retaliation. He punches Kev full-force in the face. Blood spurts out of a cut on Kev's lip, and his responding bloodstained toothy grin is creepy as hell. Kev darts forward, grabbing Kade into a headlock. Kade roars, digging his elbow in Kev's gut as he tries to work himself free.

"Oh my God!" Mom shrieks, and I whip around. The rest of the family is frozen in place at the entrance to the bar with matching slack jaws and shell-shocked expressions. "Stop them, James!" she pleads.

Dad moves forward, exuding anger and disappointment with every step. "Release your brother, Keven," he demands. Kev tightens his hold around Kade's neck, and Kade splutters as his face turns blue.

"He can't breathe!" Mom screams in a panic-laden tone. "Stop it, Keven. Please!" Tears stream down her face.

I step up beside Dad. "Kev. You're scaring Mom. Let him go."

Kev's eyes are enraged as he lifts his face to mine. He whips his head around, and his aggression lowers a notch when he locks gazes with Mom. Stepping back, he releases Kaden, shoving him away from him as if he can't bear the sight of him. Kade grasps for air, clutching a hand to his throat as he shoots daggers at Kev. He straightens up. "I'm done with you." His voice is hoarse. "Stay the hell out of my life, and I'll stay out of yours."

"Don't say I didn't warn you," Kev spits out.

Kaden walks over to Mom, forcing a neutral expression on his face. He hugs her. "It's okay, Mom. I'm okay." He presses a kiss to the top of her head as silent tears roll down her cheeks. I move back to Faye, circling my arm around her shoulder. She looks upset by this too. Dad looks like he wants to knock both their heads together as he talks in urgent whispers to Keven.

Kade wraps his arm around Mom's waist, ushering her in the direction of the hotel. Faye and I follow suit, and the rest of my brothers trail behind us. We leave Dad and Kev still talking outside the bar.

I only relax when we are back in our hotel room, away from my warring family. "What the hell was that all about?" Faye ponders, shimmying out of her jeans.

"I don't know, but I've never seen Kaden so incensed. I think he meant what he said too." I pull my shirt up over my head and unbutton my jeans.

Faye wanders into the bathroom in her shirt and panties, and my gaze roams her long, slim, tanned legs with interest. She reappears with a toothbrush in the corner of her mouth. "Keven kinda scared me tonight. The look on his face..." Her words are slightly garbled, but she doesn't need to elaborate. I get what she's saying, and I totally agree. Kev is one of the most controlled guys I know, but he has this dark center that erupts every now and then, and it ain't pretty. I don't even want to think about why it's there or what he may or may not have done up to this point. Some of the dudes he mixes with are downright scary, and not for the first time, I'm genuinely concerned for my brother.

But I don't know what to do about it.

In the past, I've raised my concerns to Kade, and he always assured me he was looking out for him. *But after tonight, who knows?* I have a feeling that things have irrevocably altered between my brothers, and that worries me more than it should.

♥♥♥♥♥♥♥

The tension is palpable the next day on the bus as we travel to County Wexford. Faye is anxious and antsy beside me, and Mom looks like she's been up half the night crying. Dad is sitting beside her today, and they are talking in quiet whispers. Kaden and Keven are sitting at opposite ends of the minibus, and they haven't uttered a word to anyone since last night.

After a few hours' drive, the bus turns off the main road, jostling alongside roads that are in ill repair and getting narrower and rougher the farther we advance. We're bumped from side to side in our seats as the bus travels on uneven terrain. "Look," Faye says, pointing straight ahead. "I can see the sea." A stunning smile lights up her face. Sure enough, we are driving closer to the blue-green waters of the Irish Sea. The bus veers a sudden left, and we sway in our seats.

"I think I'm going to hurl," Keaton announces, looking decidedly green in the face. He clamps a hand over his mouth.

"Just hold on, we're here," Faye supplies as the bus pulls up in front of an impressively sized beachfront property. The house is on two levels, and it's modern and stylish with its crisp white walls and cherry-stained wooden windows. A large balcony extends across the width of the property at the top level overlooking the vast, lush, green lawn out front. The bus draws to a complete standstill behind the two SUVs Dad rented, and we amble out. I help Dad, Kal, Keanu, and the bus driver unload our luggage while Mom greets the pretty brunette in the cream fitted pant suit waiting at the front door. Her cheeks darken as she greets us one by one, and I smirk. It's a reaction we are well used to, but it never gets old.

Faye smacks my arm.

"What?"

"Stop being so smug," she admonishes, firmly putting me back in place.

We claim one of the double rooms facing onto the rear of the property, overlooking the outdoor swimming pool. A stone path stretches from the far side of the pool down to a small wooden gate, and, I'm guessing, on to the beach beyond.

"Wow, this place is gorgeous. Your mom chose well," Faye says, quickly unpacking our stuff. We'll be staying here for the next week before we drive back to Dublin for the trip home.

I open the French doors to our private balcony, taking Faye's hand and pulling her out with me. We have our own wicker table and chairs and two loungers. I wrap my arms around her from behind as we take in the amazing view. The beach seems to stretch for miles on either side. The white silken sand and clear blue sea is as good as you'd find anywhere. Basking under streams of buttery sunshine, we could be in the Adriatic or the Caribbean, and it wouldn't beat this. Ireland has surprised me with the variety of the scenery, and the warmth and humor of the people. I can totally understand why it's such a popular tourist destination.

A loud knock raps on our door. "Are you decent?" Kal shouts out. Faye laughs, and I roll my eyes. I stalk to the door and fling it open. Kal is shading his eyes with his hand and staring purposely at the floor. "Is it safe to look?"

I swat his head. "Stop being a jerk."

His grin is teasing as he lifts his head, lounging against the doorframe. Of course, he's bare chested, and his shorts hang low on his hips. "I wouldn't have to be if you weren't so keen to get Faye naked and on her back all the time."

Faye chokes on a laugh. "You make it sound like we have sex nonstop."

His brows climb up to his hairline. "Don't you?"

"Knock it off, asshole. Was there a reason for your visit or is this just an attempt to piss me off?"

"We're going down to the beach if you want to come with. Mom's going to fix a picnic basket so we can eat there."

"Sounds good," Faye concurs.

"We'll meet you down there."

It takes us a good forty minutes to follow my brothers. Not my fault I couldn't keep my hands off Faye while she was changing into her skimpy white and gold bikini. I had her stripped and bare in mere seconds, wasting no time burying myself inside her, totally proving Kal's point—not that he's ever going to know.

We saunter down to the beach hand in hand. With her stunning looks, tall frame, long legs, and curves in all the right places, Faye could be a model if she was so inclined. Her long, dark hair is wavy and blowing softly in the gentle breeze. I lean in and kiss her mouth as we step onto the warm sand. The beach is practically deserted with the exception of another family about two hundred meters on our left and a smattering of couples in the distance to our right. There is no sign of Kade or Kev, but the rest of my brothers are here, spread-eagled on wide loungers, sipping sodas and munching on chips.

"Where's Mom and Dad?" I ask, dropping Faye's bag down on one of the empty loungers.

"Gone to the store to get stuff for the picnic," Keaton replies, swinging his legs around and sitting up on the side of his lounger. "It's fucking hot. Make sure you have sunscreen on."

"Yes, Mom."

Faye swats my head. "Keaton's right. Take your top off so I can do your back."

"You can do me anywhere you like," I quip.

Every one of my brothers groans, and Faye snorts.

"I think she already did you unless I'm mistaken about that just-got-fucked look on both your faces," Kal replies, making a rude gesture with his hands.

"Wouldn't you like to know." I smirk, and Faye swats me again.

"Knock it off," she murmurs quietly, tugging at the hem of my shirt. I yank it over my head and sit down on the side of the lounger while she applies sunscreen to my back.

Keanu hands me two sodas before stretching back on his lounger, tilting his face up to the sun.

"Right. My turn." Faye nudges me to my feet, handing the tube of sunscreen over. She pulls her flimsy white kimono off and crawls over the lounger, sitting down on the other side. Tying her hair up in a messy bun, she grants me full access to her back. Her skin is golden and lightly freckled, and I lean down and press a soft kiss to the center of her spine. She shivers, and I smile.

I warm the cream in my hands before lathering it over her back, working it completely into her skin. A little moan flies out of her mouth, and I mentally fist pump the air. I love how my touch affects her. How she squirms and shivers under my fingertips. The day she stops is the day I'll start worrying.

Kent scoffs, and I flip my attention to my younger brother. His attention is focused this way, as he eyes Faye from head to toe, and I don't like it one fucking bit. "Eyes front and center, Kent," I snap, growling at the little shit.

Kal, Keaton, and Keanu all bolt upright at my tone, glancing quickly from me to him. Faye has gone stiff underneath my hands.

"Chill the fuck out, Ky. It's not like I haven't seen a hot girl in a bikini before." He deliberately refuses to look away, smirking at me as he licks his lips provocatively, blowing a kiss at my girlfriend.

My hands ball into fists, and even though I know he's baiting me, I can't help taking a step forward. "She's not yours to look at or blow kisses at," I fume.

Faye jumps up, planting herself in front of me. "Calm down, babe. He's only fucking with you." She angles her head around in Kent's direction.

"And *you*, knock it off. I think there's been enough fighting in the last twenty-four hours without adding to it."

Surprisingly, Kent backs down without a word, and I allow Faye to drag me into the water to cool off in more ways than one.

The rest of the afternoon passes by without issue. Thank fuck. Mom and Dad join us and we enjoy lunch outside, spending the rest of the day sunbathing and swimming. Faye reads while I listen to music on my phone, our loungers pushed together and our bodies angled toward one other. Every so often, I reach out and brush her arm, squeeze her thigh, or press a kiss to her cheek, and she emits these cute little contented sighs that I love.

We return to the house when it turns cooler, and our stomachs start rumbling. Dad barbecues outside, and we chill for the rest of the night with a few beers. Kade joins us for a few hours, but Kev hasn't left his room since we arrived. Mom left to coax him into joining us, but she returned on her own with an unhappy look on her face. I want to kick my brother into next week for ruining the atmosphere and upsetting Mom, but I'm also really worried about him.

♥♥♥♥♥♥♥

When Faye's dad, Adam, arrives on our doorstep the following morning, he brings an unexpected guest. I stifle a groan as Kent's eyes swallow Whitney up whole, his grin getting bolder when she sends him a naughty look that's suggestive in the extreme.

Fuck.

Things are about to get even more complicated.

Chapter Ten

Faye

I hug Adam tightly, trying to work out how I feel about the fact my half-sister is here. I'm not sure why. Adam had told me she didn't want to come, so I don't know what has happened since we last spoke to change that. I've tried to mend bridges with Whitney on several occasions over the last few months, but she has blatantly ignored all my efforts to reach out to her. This is the first time I'm in her company since that disastrous first encounter last November. Back then, her hair was long and a shocking pink color. Now it's shorter, framed in an edgy bob that suits her, and dyed a luminous blue à la Katy Perry.

Josh—my half-brother and one of the twins—gives me a warm hug. "Hi, Faye," he says, looking reticently at all the Kennedys. Josh is a little sweetheart when you get him on his own but unbelievably shy in bigger groups. This kind of a setup is probably giving him heart palpitations.

I tuck him protectively into my side, and he's almost up to my shoulder. Both he and Jake are only nine, and they're going to be giants if they keep growing at this rate. "Look how tall you've gotten! I can't believe it's only been six weeks since I last saw you."

His smile is carefree and happy, and I squeeze him even tighter to my side. "Make sure to come up to my room later. I have something for you!" His eyes light up, and a surge of warmth invades every cell in my body. I've always wanted siblings, and the twins have welcomed me with open arms, in complete contrast to their older sister.

Jake is currently high-fiving each of my cousins and chatting animatedly to Alex. His confidence knows no bounds. The twins couldn't have more different personalities if they tried.

"Come say hi to your sister" I overhear Adam tell Whitney.

Reluctantly, she steps forward, eyeballing me through hooded lashes. "Hi, Faye," she mutters, crossing her arms over her chest as she sends me a challenging look.

So, that's how it's going to be.

Or maybe not.

I mentally count to ten, then lean down, and pull her into a hug. Shock splays across her face, and she's frozen in my arms. "I'm really glad you came." That's only half a lie. Perhaps this will give us the opportunity to get to know one another, to form a sisterly bond. She shucks out of my embrace, eying me warily. I smile. "I mean it. I'm happy you're here."

"Well, that makes one of us," she mumbles ungratefully.

"Hey, Whit," Kent says, unashamedly raking his eyes over her body. "You look hot." I dig my elbow in his ribs, subtly gesturing at Adam. Adam doesn't miss a thing, and while he's presently chatting to Alex, I'm certain he has one ear on this conversation.

"Kent." Whitney purses her lips in a failed attempt to hide her obvious pleasure at his comment.

Ky comes up beside me, placing his hand on my lower back. "Whitney." He nods at my sister. "I trust I don't need to have a repeat of the last conversation we had."

Her eyes narrow to slits. "Screw your demands. You're not the boss of me." She thrusts her hands on her slim hips. "No one is."

Kent smirks, and Ky turns his death glare on him. "I'm sure I don't need to remind you that she's underage and you need to behave."

"Fuck you, Ky. Go join the oldies." He gestures to where Adam, Alex, James, and Kaden are deep in conversation. "I'm sure you'll fit right in."

I drag Ky away before it turns into World War Three. "There's no point stating the obvious, Ky. He's not going to listen to you, and she sure as hell isn't. We'll just have to keep an eye on them." I don't trust Kent around my sister, at all, but calling him out on it will only make him more determined.

Ky grunts, retrieving his vibrating phone from his pocket. He frowns at the screen. "It's Brad. I better take this." He disappears into the house as Alex ushers everyone out to the pool area.

Adam and my brothers and sister are spending the day with us today as prearranged, but they are actually staying at his parents' house a few miles away. I'm due to meet them all there tomorrow for lunch. It will be my first time meeting my grandparents although I have spoken to them a couple of times on the phone.

"Your grandparents are very excited to finally meet you," Adam tells me as we lie side by side on adjoining loungers around the pool.

"I'm looking forward to meeting them too." I offer him a brittle smile as my stomach lurches to my toes.

He chuckles, reaching out to pat my arm. "There's no need to be nervous, honey. They already love you."

I scratch an imaginary scab on my arm. "I've never had grandparents before. I'm not sure how I should act."

He sits up, leaning his elbows on his knees. "Just be yourself. Honestly, there's no need to be nervous. My parents are very laid-back and looking forward to getting to know you." He claws a hand through his dark hair, and I spy a few strands of gray that weren't there before. "You can bring Kyler if that'll help."

I immediately perk up. "I can?"

He chuckles again. "Of course. I pretty much took it as a given that he was coming."

"Okay. I'll ask him."

"I'm happy to come with," Ky says, looming over me with a smile. "Sorry, I didn't mean to eavesdrop." He hands me a drink, offering a second one to Adam.

"You're sure?" My hand curls around his wrist.

He sits on the edge of my bed. "I'll do whatever you want, babe. You know that."

Adam chuckles. "I see you've said goodbye to your balls, Kyler."

"Dad!" I shriek, utterly gobsmacked. Adam is usually pretty strait-laced, so to hear those words coming out of his mouth is a shock to the system.

His Adam's apple jumps in his throat as he stares at me, eyes brimming with emotion.

I bite down on my lower lip. "What?" I look between him and Ky, totally perplexed. Ky's expression is tender as he tucks my hair behind my ear.

"You called me Dad," Adam whispers.

I did? Oh my gosh, I did. It was totally unconscious. Completely natural. My chest tightens at the look of utter delight on Adam's face. I sit up, clearing my throat. "It just slipped out," I whisper back, averting my eyes. "You don't mind?"

Reaching out, he clasps my hands, and I raise my eyes to meet his. "Mind? Sweetheart, it feels like I've been waiting an eternity for you to call me that." His shrewd eyes probe mine. "Are *you* okay with it?"

I look to Ky, and the reassurance in his eyes gives me the confidence I need. Slowly, I nod. "Yes, I think I am."

Dad moves over to my lounger, wrapping his arm around my back and pulling me into his side. I rest my head on his shoulder. Ky blows me a kiss as he walks away, giving us privacy. Adam presses a tender kiss to my head. "I'm really glad we're getting to spend this time together. It always feels so rushed when we meet for weekends. I'm looking forward to spending quality time together this week."

"Me too."

Out of the corner of my eye, I spy Whitney observing us with a sad look on her face. When she catches me watching, she spins on her heel, stomping off into the house. Adam sighs. "Is she okay?" I ask, shucking out from under his arm.

He scrubs his jaw. "I don't know. She won't talk to me. Won't talk to her mother. I don't have a clue what's going on in her head."

"But she's here. That's got to mean something."

He nods. "I hope so. Perhaps she might confide in you?"

I peer into his hopeful, concerned blue eyes. "I think I might be the problem."

He shakes his head. "You may be part of it, but there's more going on with her. I wish I knew how to help her."

He sounds so worried, so helpless, and the words just fly out of my mouth without any encouragement. "I'll try and talk to her, and I'll keep an eye on her. You don't need to worry. I'll watch out for her."

Little did I realize what I was getting myself into.

♥♥♥♥♥♥♥

The oldies are happy to stay in the house tonight, so we've decide to get a taxi into Wexford town to go dancing. Kev is refusing to come, which puts a bit of a dampener on things, but I'm not going to let his stubbornness ruin the night. I'm in our bedroom, applying my makeup, when there's a knock on my door, and Whitney calls out my name.

"Come in," I say, wondering why she's deemed to grace me with her presence.

I perch on the corner of the bed, looking up at her as I wait for her to clue me in. "I need your help," she says, startling the heck out of me.

"Okay."

"I want to go out with you tonight, but Dad said no. I was hoping you'd talk to him for me."

Even though she's probably only using me, I can't help feeling happy that she's come to me about this. *This is the sort of thing you ask of your older sister, right?* This could go some way toward breaking the wall down between us. I stand up. "If I do this, you have to promise to stay by my side. I'm not giving, um, Dad, my word that I'll look out for you if you are planning to ignore me all night." I level a stern look at her, watching her pout deepen.

"But—"

"No buts. And no sneaking off to hook up with Kent either. There's no way you're doing that on my watch." I plant my hands on my hips.

Her eyes narrow, and I can tell she'd love to let rip at me. But she can't. Not when she needs my help. Her foot taps off the ground, and I can almost see the wheels churning in her head. "What if I—"

"Nope. Those are my terms."

"Fine," she huffs, crossing her arms.

"Okay. Let me finish getting ready, and I'll talk to him then."

She strides toward the door, failing to keep the excitement off her face. At the last second, she turns around. "Um, thanks," she mumbles, looking at her feet. Wow, miracles will never cease.

It takes a lot more than anticipated to get Adam to agree, but, finally, he relents. Whitney barely reacts when I tell her, having had time to compose herself since our last chat. I roll my eyes as Ky takes my hand, leading me outside to the taxi. "I hope you know what you're doing," he whispers. "This could be a complete disaster."

"I know," I sigh, getting in the backseat beside him. "But there's no backing out now."

♥♥♥♥♥♥♥

The venue is set over three levels with the nightclub part residing on the top floor. We have a couple of drinks in the bar downstairs before making our way upstairs. Slick beats boom over the loudspeakers as we enter the club. The place is jam-packed, and the dance floor is a hot mess of writhing bodies. Couples are making out everywhere, and Kent rubs his hands together. "Hells yeah. This is my kind of place."

"Let's dance," Whitney suggests, grabbing his hand without waiting for his reply. She yanks him out into the middle of the dance floor where we can't see.

"And here we go," Ky drawls.

I sigh. "This is going to be a long night."

"Lighten up, you two," Kal says. "They can't get into too much trouble here." He points at a booth to his left. "Kade reserved that one for us. We are right by the door, so if they try to sneak off for any kinky fuckery, we'll spot them."

I punch Kal in the arm. "Do not even joke about such a thing."

"Have another drink or ten," he mocks. "Just chill the fuck out. Besides, Kent isn't a total idiot. He won't do anything to risk things between you and your dad."

"Are we talking about the same Kent? The one who knows no boundaries and does what the hell he wants whenever he wants?" My tone betrays my incredulity.

"Ouch." Kal winces. "Don't let Kent hear you have such a low opinion of him. You'll hurt his feelings."

"If he has any," Ky remarks.

"Oh, he's got plenty. Why do you think he acts like he does?" Kal throws that statement out before making a beeline for the bar.

The next couple of hours pass by in a haze of drinking and dancing. Whitney and Kent are stuck to each other like glue, and they barely stop kissing to come up for air. However, they have stayed near us, and there's zero groping going on, so I'm happy. They move off the dance floor as a slow song starts up, heading toward our booth where Kal, Kaden, Keanu, and Keaton are chatting to a bunch of rough-looking dudes. Ky reels me into his arms. "I don't like the look of them," I murmur, subtly nodding at the table.

"Kade will lock it down if necessary. Relax, babe. You're worrying too much."

The instant his hot mouth presses against my neck all responsible thoughts fly out of my head. Pulling me in even closer to his body, he smashes his hips against mine, demonstrating how turned on he is. "I love dancing with you," he rasps, nibbling on my earlobe. "You're such a sexy dancer."

"You're not so bad yourself." I gasp when his hand squeezes my ass. "Ky." I send him a cautionary look. "We're in public."

"I know, babe." His tongue licks a line up the side of my neck, and now I'm the one grabbing him to me, my hands slipping under his shirt, exploring the contours of his muscular back. "But I can't control myself around you. Not when you look so fucking gorgeous and I want to rip the clothes off your back and bury myself deep inside you."

"Oh, God." I groan. "What the hell are you doing to me?"

"I know what I'd like to be doing to you," he teases, tracing his lips along my collarbone. An intense shiver ripples through me, and my knees buckle. All semblance of control evaporates. Grabbing his hand, I take him with me as I stride toward the bathrooms. There are no separate bathrooms here, just a row of individual unisex toilets with their own door. The one on the end is currently unoccupied, and I run toward it before someone can beat me to it.

Ky laughs quietly. "I like your thinking." He pulls me inside, locks the door, and then pushes me up against the wall. His eyes are dark with lust, and the ache between my legs intensifies. "I'm so fucking hard I think I might combust," he admits, slipping his hand under my dress and caressing the inside of my thigh. I grip his shoulders, shivering and quivering under his expert ministrations. His fingers brush over my knickers, and I suck in a gasp. Slowly and deliberately, he rolls my dress up to my waist. He cups me there, and a downright wicked look repaints his face. Lightning fast, he rips my knickers off, pulling them down my legs in one expert move. I'm frantically popping buttons on his jeans at the same time, whipping them down his legs along with his boxers.

He slides one finger inside me. "Always so ready," he whispers, slamming his mouth down on mine with urgent need. I claw at his back, fisting my hand in his shirt as I pull him to me. He lifts my thigh up and enters me in one confident thrust. I moan into his mouth, as blissful tremors invade every inch of my body. He pushes me in farther to the wall, and I wrap both legs around his waist. My fingers dig into his shoulders as he pumps into me. He holds me up with one hand, the other braced on the side of the wall. The door rattles as he thrusts into me harder and faster, and I dig my fingers into his back, biting his shoulder to smother the urge to scream from the top of my lungs. Every part of my body is on fire, and I can't get enough. Every time with Ky feels different than the last time, and I love how he makes me feel so much. My core throbs almost painfully, and I know I'm close already. This is naughty and dirty and I'm loving it. Perhaps it's the taboo factor or the thought that people outside must know what we're doing, but it doesn't take me long to reach climax. Ky covers my mouth with his, capturing my moans and screams, grunting as his own release consumes him.

Sweat rolls down my back, adhering my dress to my skin. Ky rests his head on my shoulder, and I run my fingers through the silky strands of his hair. "That was so hot," I croak, struggling to get my breath and my voice back on track.

"Damn straight." I can hear the grin in his tone.

Slowly, he lifts his head, and his gaze collides with mine. We stare at one another, and it's as if he can see inside me, straight through to my soul. When I look in his eyes I detect the extent of his devotion, and my heart swells to bursting point. No one will ever love me as much as Kyler

Kennedy. "I love you, Faye." He kisses me sweetly, in complete contrast to the way he just dominated me.

"And I love you." I cup his face, and my heart is full with so many emotions.

With great tenderness, he eases my legs down onto the ground. After cleaning me up, he snatches my knickers off the floor, helping me step into them, before smoothing my dress into place. He is tucking himself back in his jeans when the sounds of banging greet my ears.

"Faye! Ky!"

The hammering grows closer and more insistent as I lock eyes with my boyfriend. Kal calls out our names again, along with a few choice expletives. Chills snake up and down my spine at the undeniable panic in his voice.

Ky buttons his jeans up and takes my hand, opening the door just as Kal reaches it. Kal smirks momentarily, scanning our flushed faces. Just as quickly, the smirk withers and dies.

I put gentle pressure on his arm. "What is it? What's happened? Is Whitney okay?" It's the most logical assumption.

His lips pull into a grim line. "We have a problem."

Chapter Eleven

Kyler

"What kind of problem?" I ask, steering Faye out of the bathroom and ushering her into the main room.

"A Kent and Whitney disappearing act kind of problem." Kal confirms our worst fears.

"Surely, they can't have gone far. They are probably just outside making out like bandits." Faye's tone sounds hopeful, but she looks crestfallen and panicked. I place my hand on her lower back, rubbing soothing circles with my thumb.

Kal grimaces, and my chest tightens. "What don't I know?"

He gulps. "We think they've gone with those guys we were talking to."

"What?" Faye shrieks, almost piercing my eardrums. "They looked dodgy as fuck! How could you let them go with them?!"

Kal rubs the back of his neck. "We didn't *let* them leave. They gave us the slip."

Faye throws her hands in the air. "We were gone for, like, ten minutes, and you lost them. Great." Her voice drips with sarcasm.

"Hey, hang on here a sec, Faye. No one said we were on babysitting duty, and we weren't the ones having a sneaky fuck in the bathroom."

"Kal." My tone cuts through him. He will not speak to Faye like that even if it's the truth.

He holds up his hands. "Look, let's not argue. We need to figure out where they've gone." His cell pings as he leads us back to the table.

"How the hell did this happen?" I ask Kade.

He sighs, running a hand through his hair. "Those guys latched on to us, and they wouldn't take the hint, but I wasn't going to tell them to fuck off either. At least two of them were high and acting weird."

"Oh God." Faye looks like she's going to puke.

I tuck her into my side. "It's okay. We'll find them." I urge Kade to continue with my eyes.

"They invited us back to their place, but we declined. Then Kal went to the bar with Keats, and myself and Keanu went to the toilet, and when we came back, they were all gone. I've texted Kent but he's ignoring me. Do you have Whitney's cell number?" he asks Faye.

She grabs her purse, extracting her phone. "Fuck!" Her chest heaves. "I'm out of charge."

"Okay. No one panic. I have a lock on Kent's location," Kal says, and Faye exhales in relief.

"Kev?" I ask, jumping to the obvious conclusion. Kal nods. Dad insisted years ago that monitoring devices were embedded in all our cells. At first, I was disgusted at the lack of privacy, but over the course of the last year, there have been plenty of occasions when I've been grateful for his foresight. Now is definitely one of those times. "Let's go."

We head outside and flag down a taxi. This one only takes four passengers, so we make Keanu and Keaton promise to take a separate taxi home, and then the rest of us bail in. Kal shows the driver his phone, and he heads off in the right direction.

Faye is trembling beside me, and I wrap her solidly in my arms. "Try not to worry. Kent won't let anyone hurt Whitney." Unless he's overpowered or outnumbered, but I don't voice those thoughts.

"What the hell were they thinking? What if something happens to them before we get there?"

"We'll get there in time, and they aren't that far ahead of us." I hope.

We head out of the busy town, traversing quieter roads. When the driver turns off a poorly lit road onto a narrow dirt track that looks like it's in the middle of nowhere, my panic starts to kick in. There are no streetlamps on this road, and we are surrounded by acres and acres of unoccupied green fields. In the background, the perimeter of a large, dense forest offers no comfort. The taxi bumps along the track, and even the driver is looking nervously around which doesn't bode well. Kade and I lock eyes over Faye's head, and he shares my concern.

"It looks like they've stopped," Kal says in a clipped tone, showing the driver the phone.

He nods. "It should be around the next bend."

The car trundles up the road. As we turn the corner, a dim glow appears in the distance. I squint in the darkness just about making out the blurry structure of a building. We get closer, and the building becomes more solid. The house is two stories with a stone façade and a thatched roof. Scaffolding on one side suggests a work in construction. Kal turns around, gulping as he pins me with an apprehensive look.

"Please stop here," Kade instructs the driver when we're about three hundred meters away. He pulls out a hundred-dollar euro note, stuffing it in the man's fist. "If you wait here for us, I'll double that."

"Not necessary," Kal cuts in. "Kev is on his way. He snuck out and borrowed one of the cars."

We get out, and Kade thanks the man, sending him on his way.

"Okay," Kade says, assuming command. "Ky and I will go to the house. You two wait here for Kev."

Kal and Faye both start protesting at once. Kade silences them with a black look. "I don't give a fuck what you want. I don't like this. Don't like it at all." He looks anxious and wound up tight. All I can see for miles are green fields and trees. No one is coming to help out here.

"I don't like it either which is why it's not safe to separate," Faye argues. "We're not hanging around out here in the dark while you two go up to that house on your own. There's safety in numbers."

"She has a point," Kal says.

I rub a tense spot between my brows as I stare into my girlfriend's face. "I don't want anything to happen to you."

"And I don't want anything to happen to you," she counters.

"I can take care of myself." Oh boy, that was so the wrong thing to say.

She sends me one of her special death glares, and I almost chuckle. It's been some time since I've been on the receiving end of one of those. Planting her hands on her hips, she narrows her eyes and tosses her hair over her shoulder. "I know how to take care of myself. Have you forgotten how I—"

I clamp my hand over her mouth. "I don't need to be reminded of the two times you almost died, thank you very much."

She huffs, stepping away from me with fury radiating in her eyes. "That's my sister and my cousin up there." She points at the house in the distance. "And if you don't let us come, we'll just follow you."

Kal salutes her, and Kade is reluctantly smirking. "Fine. Let them come." He turns and starts walking. "We don't have time to debate this."

I walk quickly to Faye's side, lacing my fingers in hers. Thankfully, she doesn't let the argument linger, squeezing my hand firmly in hers. We are quiet as we walk on muddy, uneven ground toward the house. Faye stumbles a little in her heels, but I keep a steady grip on her. Faint sounds of music greet us as we draw nearer. Lights are on in two of the rooms downstairs, but the rest of the house is in complete darkness. Kent's laugh rings out, trickling through the open window. Several other voices join in the laughter, and some of my tension lifts. Maybe we're big-dealing this without reason.

Kade raises a hand when we reach the corner of the house. "Let me scout it out," he whispers, holding up a hand.

He creeps stealthily along the wall toward the larger of the open windows. Streams of light cast shadows on the muddy ground outside. Kade stops at the edge of the window, straightening up with his back flat to the wall. Faye's grip on my hand tightens. Kade whips his head around, taking a quick peek into the room. More laughter rings out, as Kade sneaks back to us.

"There's six guys and Whitney and Kent," he whispers. "They're sitting in a circle on the floor, drinking and chatting. It looks chill but you can't always tell with guys like that. I think we should just knock on the door, go in for a bit, then make our excuses, and leave."

I nod in agreement. "Text Kev," I tell Kal. "Let him know the plan."

We follow Kade past the window to the front door. We've already been spotted, and the door opens the instant we reach it. A tall, skinny guy with red hair and the makings of a beard grins at us. "Changed your mind, fellas?" His toothy grin turns lecherous when he spots Faye. "Hey, gorgeous." He winks, opening the door wide. "Our door is always open for the likes of you."

"Thanks," she says, offering him a fake smile. "Does that invitation extend to my boyfriend too?"

The grin slips off his face as he finally takes notice of me. It takes colossal effort to appear pleasant when I want to smash my fist in his lewd face. "Guess so," he mutters, stepping aside.

Faye walks confidently into the house, and I've got to admire her lady balls. Kade and Kal nod at the guy as they walk in.

Kent looks up, with what looks suspiciously like relief on his face, when we step into the living room. I think the little shit has bitten off more than he can chew on this occasion. Apart from a couch and a small coffee table, there is no furniture in the room. Nail guns, tubs of paint, paintbrushes, tape, and other decorating paraphernalia are scattered on top of the newly varnished hardwood floors.

A stocky dude with shocking white-blond hair gets up, eyeing us warily. "Who the fuck are ye?"

The other four guys don't budge from their positions on the ground as they pass a joint between them. One of the men is lying flat on his back, staring at the ceiling with a glazed look on his face. The other three look sharp enough, watching proceedings with an intensity that concerns me.

"Hey man," Kal says, sauntering forward. "We met you back in the club, remember?"

The guy's pupils are dilated and unfocused as he takes us all in. You could cut the tension with a knife. Whitney is perched on the edge of the couch, a look of abject terror on her face. Faye walks to her side, dropping down beside her and circling her arm around her back. Whitney's shoulders relax a little.

"You know each other?" the same guy asks, pointing a stubby finger at the girls.

"We're sisters," Faye explains, eyeballing him head-on.

He rubs a hand over his flabby belly, and his eyes light up. "Is that so?" His gaze bounces between them. "You don't look alike."

"We have different mothers," Faye confirms, starting to look a little uncomfortable. This guy exudes dangerous vibes, and she's picking up on that.

Kent scrambles to his feet, angling his body so his back is to the guys. "You didn't need to come pick us up, but thanks, man." He slaps Kade on the back. "Save me calling a taxi. Signal's not the best out here."

The weird blond dude steps forward, slapping Kent forcefully on the back. "You're not leaving so soon, my man. We haven't shown you any of our legendary Irish hospitality."

Yeah, I'd rather not hang around to discover what that's about.

The red-haired skinny dude sits down on the edge of the sofa, and Whitney almost jumps out of her skin. I watch Faye discreetly squeeze her side in warning.

"Thanks, but we're leaving," I tell him, crossing my arms over my chest.

The blond guy cocks his head to the side, walking toward me. He puts his face all up in mine. "You'll leave when I say ye'll leave."

"Don't touch me!" Whitney shrieks, and I turn around. The red-haired guy has his hand on her bare thigh.

Faye reaches over, grabbing his hand and thrusting it away. "You heard my sister. Keep your paws to yourself."

"You're feisty." He grins. In this light, I can make out the brown nicotine stains on his teeth, and it turns my stomach as he leans around Whitney, putting his face all up in Faye's. Kade shoots me a warning look. I know Faye can look after herself, but it kills me to stand here and say nothing, do nothing. "I like my women feisty." Reaching out, he grabs a fistful of her hair, tugging her toward him. His gaze wanders down the front of her dress, and I'm done.

Yanking his hand out of her hair, I push him back forcefully. "Get your fucking hands off her!" I snap. He loses balance, tumbling off the couch.

Three of the guys get up off the floor, and I sense them moving into place behind me.

"Now that wasn't very nice, and here we are just trying to be hospitable." The blond dude plants himself in front of me. His breath is pungent as it blows across my face.

"We appreciate that," Kade says, stepping in between us. "Maybe another time. We've got to get going."

The guy turns his attention toward Kade. "You deaf or something?"

Kade locks eyes with me, and I nod. Reaching out, I take Faye's hand, urging her up. Whitney stands with her, clinging to her side, quaking and on the verge of tears.

"Mikey," he bellows over his shoulder. "Fix our guests a snack. We can't send them on their way empty-handed."

Mikey heads into the next room without a word, as the blond dude returns his focus to the girls. "What's an Irish girl doing with a bunch of yanks anyway?"

The redhead hops up, flexing his fists as he glowers at me.

"It's a long story." Faye attempts a laugh, but I can tell it's forced. Her earlier confidence is fading as realization dawns, but she needn't worry—I'm not going to let anything happen to her again. I still feel huge guilt over what went down at the diner and the cabin, and keeping her safe is my number one priority now.

"I have all the time in the world," he replies, unashamedly assessing her body from head to toe. I want to pummel his face into next week, but I control the urge. One false move and this situation detonates.

"Ronan!" Mikey pops his head out of the next room, slanting a look at the blond asshole. "I can't find the bread knife."

Ronan wets his lips. "Well, isn't that strange." He pins a suspicious look on Kent. "You wouldn't happen to know anything about that, would you?"

Kent shakes his head, looking innocent and clueless. "No idea, bro."

Ronan turns around, twirling a lock of Whitney's hair around his finger. "What about you, baby?"

She gulps, vehemently shaking her head.

"Well, I guess there's no cheese sandwiches tonight." Ronan winks at Faye. "Unless you're into meat. Plenty of meat ones to go around." He grabs his crotch, watching her face for a reaction.

Faye visibly pales. "Not if you were the last man on Earth."

Bile travels up my throat. I send a subtle communication to Kade with my eyes, and he nods tersely. We'll have to fight our way out of here no matter what. I'd rather get this shit show over and done with. There are four of us to four of them, and I like our chances. The dude passed out on the floor doesn't count nor does the redhead; I'd squash him with one punch.

Ronan laughs. "Philip is right. You're feisty." His eyes narrow in on Whitney. "But personally, I prefer the more innocent, virginal types. Although, judging by the way you were grinding against the yank on the dance floor, I'd say you know what you're doing. What about it, hot stuff, you want a ride on my dick?" Licking his lips, he thrusts his crotch forward, and a tiny sob leaks out of Whitney's mouth.

I gesture to Kade and Kal, but before we can make a move, Faye swings into action. Shoving Whitney behind her, she glares at Ronan, eying him disdainfully from head to toe. "Listen here, shit for brains." She prods him in the chest. "You don't get to speak to my sister like that. You don't get to threaten my boyfriend. We're leaving and you're not going to do a thing about it."

Ronan throws back his head, laughing. "Is that right?" He laughs again, and Faye's nostrils flare. Out of the corner of my eye, I see two of the guys moving toward the nail guns. Kal and Kent move in closer to us. "Keep going, baby," he teases. "This is turning me on."

Faye looks down, grimacing at the discernible bulge in his jeans, before jutting her chin up. "You're a creep, and you deserve this." Super fast, she brings her knee up, jamming it into his crotch. He buckles, emitting a painful roar as his knees give way. Faye brings the heel of her stilettos down on his foot, and he roars again.

The two guys race toward the nail guns as I yell. "Out! Now!"

Kent grabs Whitney, and I take Faye's arm, shoving her toward the door. The redhead rushes toward us, and Kade punches him in the face. He crumples to the floor, instantly unconscious.

Kent pulls the door open, yanking Whitney's shoes off and lifting her up into his arms. Before I can attempt the same, Faye has whipped her heels off, and she takes off running in her bare feet.

"Run!" Kade screams, barreling out the door behind Kal. Lights flash up ahead as a car approaches, and I'm praying to God that's Kev.

"Duck!" Kade roars, and I grab onto Faye before throwing us onto the ground. Mud splatters our faces, as nails whizz over our heads. Kent and Whitney are on the ground in front of us. Kent is protecting her with his body, and she's sobbing uncontrollably. Grunts and slaps echo from behind, and I cautiously glance over my shoulder. Kal and Kade are throwing punches at the two guys, trying to wrestle the nail guns away from them. "Get the girls out of here!" Kade throws out.

Kent and I move almost simultaneously, helping the girls to their feet. Kent carries a sobbing Whitney in his arms as I take Faye's hand and we run toward the approaching headlights.

The SUV comes to a halt, and Kev opens the door, frowning when he sees the state of us. "Where are the others?"

"We're here," Kade shouts from somewhere behind us.

I help Faye into the backseat while Kent does the same, locking the seatbelt around Whitney. Her sobs have transformed to sniffles. When her eyes roll back in her head, I realize she's smashed. As soon as Kade and Kal are in the car, Kev floors the engine, reversing back down the path with skillful speed.

"What happened back there?" I ask.

"We got the upper hand, grabbed the nail guns, and threw them into a field on our way to the car," Kade replies.

"Fucking hell. That was cutting it close." Kal swings his head in Kent's direction. "What the fuck were you thinking, you idiot!?"

"I had it under control." Kent huffs, feigning indifference. He trails his hand up and down Whitney's arm in a soothing gesture.

"Like fuck you did." My eyes narrow to slits. "Of all the stupid shit you've pulled, that takes the cake. That blond asshole was a crazy fucker. He could've hurt Whitney."

A crazy ass grin appears on Kent's face as he reaches a hand behind him. "And I would have cut his fucking throat if he dared lay a hand on her," he admits, brandishing a long kitchen knife. "We weren't unprotected."

I slam a hand into my palm. "You stole their knife?! Of course, you did." I shake my head, muttering under my breath. God only knows what would've happened if he'd produced that back at the house.

Kal splutters. "I don't know who is crazier, you or those assholes. Damn, Kent."

Kent grins like he's just gotten a pat on the back.

"Do not encourage that shit, Kal," I hiss.

"Stop the car!" Whitney shrieks. "I'm going to be sick."

Kade and Kev exchange looks for the first time in days. Kev brings the car to a juddering halt. "Make it snappy, Whitney. We're not far enough away yet for my comfort."

Kent helps Whitney out of the car, but she pushes him aside. "I want Faye."

Faye climbs out of the car and goes to her sister. Holding her hair back, she keeps an arm around Whitney's back as she empties her stomach. Kent and I keep watch, our eyes fixated on the road we've just traveled, watching for any sign that we've been followed, but all I can see is eerie darkness. The longer we're out here, the more anxious I become. "We need to leave, girls." I step closer. "Are you okay for a bit, Whitney? At least until we hit the main road?" I'll feel safer when we reach civilization.

She nods. "I'm okay."

Faye helps her back into the car, sitting beside her. Whitney rests her head on her shoulder and closes her eyes. Kent gets in beside me, and no one speaks as Kev drives us back to the house.

Chapter Twelve

Faye

Whitney is unnaturally quiet the entire journey back to the house. She clings to my side like a limpet, and I'm worried about her. This is not Whitney's usual MO. The original plan was for her to return to our grandparents' house, but I can't let her go there in the state she's in. Besides smelling of vomit and alcohol, she's also covered in mud, and her face is blotchy from crying.

Kev confirmed our dad is still back at the house with Alex and James which surprised me. Apparently, he dropped the twins back at his house and came back for drinks with a few of his friends. Still, at this late hour, I thought they would be long gone.

I'm trying to figure out how I can sneak Whitney into the house and clean her up without Adam noticing when Kev swings into our driveway.

"What the actual fuck?" Kal exclaims, sitting bolt upright in his seat. I sit up straighter, stretching my neck as I peer out the front window. My eyes almost bug out of my head at the sight of my dad and my uncle throwing punches at one another out in front of the house while Alex looks on from the doorway.

Great.

As if this night couldn't get any worse.

For flip's sake, they're acting like rowdy teenagers. *And James has the nerve to criticize his sons for the crap they get into?*

"Kent!" I hiss, leaning across the back seat. "Take Whitney up to my room and find something in my wardrobe for her to change into. We'll get out first, and when they're distracted, duck around the side of the house and go in the back entrance. I'll meet you up there in a few."

"'Kay. I'll look after her."

I snort, because he's done such an outstanding job so far tonight. He narrows his eyes but wisely bites his tongue.

Ky climbs out of the car the instant Kev brings it to a standstill. I jump out after him. Alex is beseeching the men to stop, hovering in front of the door, clasping and unclasping her hands, her eyes all panicky and pissed. She breathes a sigh of relief when she spots us approaching. "Oh, thank God. Kaden, please fix this. They're not listening to me."

I walk over to Alex's side, looping my arm through hers. "How did this happen?" She takes a step back, looking me up and down. I'm covered in mud and I know I'm a right state. "Don't even ask."

She scans her boys as I watch Kent sneak Whitney around the side of the house unnoticed. Alex shakes her head but lets it go. "Honestly, I'm not surprised. It's clearly in their genes." She flings her hands in the air, pinning James with an incredulous look.

It's completely irrational to see two grown men going at it like wild animals. To be fair, most punches hit the air rather than each other, but still. James growls at something Adam says before Kaden plants himself in between them, talking in a low tone of voice. The other boys stand around the edges, waiting to see how things pan out.

"Why are they fighting?" I ask, slipping my ruined heels off and leaving them at the front door. Alex averts her eyes, looking everywhere but at me. "Please tell me," I ask quietly.

She lifts her head, and her face is full of compassion. "It's only because he's drunk." I beseech her with my eyes. "Your father tried to kiss me, and James took offense."

My brain is frazzled, and I blink profusely as I stare at her with my mouth hanging open. "What?"

She smooths a hand over her hair. "We've all had too much to drink. Everything was going great until your dad's friends left. Because it was so late, he decided to wait around for Whitney, so that only left the three of us. James went to the bathroom, and your father and I were talking, and he leaned in to kiss me just as James stepped back into the room. He went ballistic, hauling Adam out here, and they started going at it."

The lump in my throat almost chokes me but not enough to dampen my curiosity. "Did you want to kiss my dad?" I eyeball her.

She instantly shakes her head, grimacing a little. "No, sweetheart. Your father is a lovely man, but I don't have those kinds of feelings for him. To be fair, I don't think he has them for me either. Like I said, drink makes you act stupidly sometimes."

The men have stopped fighting now. Keven and Kaden are talking with James, while Ky and Kal talk to Adam. "What a total fuck-up," I mutter.

"We'll fix everything tomorrow. Don't worry, sweetheart. It'll all be fine." I think she's trying to convince herself as much as me.

Ky steps up to us. "Can you get Whitney, please? Kev is going to drive your dad and sister home."

"Okay." Silently, I mouth "Stay with your mom."

I race up the stairs and burst into my room. Whitney is sitting on our bed with her knees tucked into her chest, staring straight ahead. Her hair is sopping wet, and she's only wearing a bath towel. Kent is rummaging in my wardrobe. "You put her in the shower?" I ask, lifting a brow.

"She smelled like puke, and she was filthy. I had no choice. Don't worry, I kept my eyes on the ground." I pin him with a disbelieving look. He curses. "You must think I'm a total douche if you assume I'd take advantage of a situation like this." He doesn't look happy at the thought.

"It's okay. I believe you, and thank you for looking after her. We need to get her downstairs. Can you make her a coffee and grab a bottle of water while I help her get dressed?"

"Sure." He takes a quick look at Whitney, pausing as if he wants to say something, before shaking his head and slipping out of the room.

I pull a short black dress out of my wardrobe that's a close enough match to the one she was wearing tonight. Hopefully, Adam won't notice. I remove my hairdryer and walk to the bed. "Whitney, we need to hurry up. Dad is waiting for you."

"I don't have the energy," she mumbles.

"Is it okay if I do it?"

She shrugs, and I take that as my cue. I quickly blow dry her hair, thankful she cut it, and run a facial wipe over her face before helping her into the dress. I pull a pair of flip-flops out of my wardrobe and slip them on her feet. "Faye," she whispers. "Why are you being so nice to me?"

I stop what I'm doing, straightening up so I'm looking her in the eye. "You're my sister. This is what sisters do." My brow furrows. "I think."

"Oh." She looks disappointed in my answer, and that disappoints me.

I place soft hands on her shoulder. "Kent should never have taken you there tonight. I was extremely worried that something had happened to you. I would never have forgiven myself if you'd been hurt." I bite the inside of my mouth. "I know we don't know each other very well, but I'm really hoping we can rectify that. I'm not your enemy, Whitney. I just want to be your friend." The vulnerable look on her face unravels me. The usual front Whitney presents is far easier to deal with. I'm out of my comfort zone with this Whitney, but I like it. I feel like I'm finally getting a glimpse at the girl who is my sister. Behind all the bravado, and the attention-seeking behavior, she's drowning. "I've always wanted a sister," I continue. "And I'd really like it if we could try to be that to one another."

She gulps and a lone tear drips down her face as Kent knocks on the door. "Give us a minute," I call out. I brush her tear away with my thumb. "I'm always available if you want to talk, about anything or nothing."

"All the people I let in leave me," she whispers, and a part of my heart breaks.

"I have some experience of that."

She nods slowly. "Thank you. For coming after me. For getting me out of there."

I smile. "I'd do it again to keep you safe. I'm glad nothing happened."

"Can I come in yet?" Kent grumbles from the corridor, and we share a smile.

"You like him?" I ask.

She shrugs. "I guess so."

I let Kent in and he keeps his arm around Whitney's shoulder while she takes timid sips of her coffee. Ky appears in the doorframe. "We need to move things along before round two kicks off downstairs."

"I'm ready." Whitney hands me her mug, looking more composed and a lot more sober than when she arrived. "I'll see you tomorrow at the house."

I nod. She starts to walk away, but I pull her into a quick hug. "See you tomorrow."

Her cheeks redden as Kent guides her out of the room.

Ky strips off his muddy shirt, tossing it on the floor. "What a night."

I shimmy out of my dress, yawning. "You're telling me. Why can't we ever seem to go out without some bloody drama occurring?"

He snorts. "Forget it, babe. That's never going to happen. Drama is our middle name."

♥♥♥♥♥♥

We all sleep in the following morning, and I'm grateful that we have limited time before we have to leave for my grandparents' house. The stress hovering over everyone like a dark cloud is claustrophobic. Kaden and Keven seem to have retreated to their earlier position, and they're not talking again. Alex is giving a sheepish-looking James her best stink-eyed look, and both of them are clearly nursing hangovers from hell. The rest of us are tiptoeing around the elephant in the room.

Until Kal saunters into the kitchen.

Kal can always be counted on to say what needs to be said.

Yawning, he drags a hand through his hair which is currently sticking up in all directions. He yanks the fridge door open, removing the juice. Chugging from the carton, he turns around, stalling as he surveys all the glum expressions. "Don't stop the party on my account," he drawls. He tosses the empty juice carton in the bin before sauntering to the table.

"So, I'm curious." He slings an arm around Alex's shoulder. "Did Adam try to slip you the tongue, or was it more of a peck on the lips?"

Alex shakes her head, as coffee sprays from my uncle's mouth. "Stop it, Kalvin," she pleads. "You're only going to make things worse."

A serious expression washes over his face. "That's where you're wrong, Mom. Not discussing things, and keeping secrets, almost killed us in the past. Pretending it didn't happen won't make it go away."

"This is for your mother and me to resolve," James says, standing up. "But I appreciate the sentiment, son."

Ky and I exchange surprised expressions. "You're wrong," I add. "This involves my dad too, and it's more than just what happened last night." Ky squeezes my thigh under the table in a show of support. "I hate the thought I'll have to keep both sides of my family separate, which is the reality if you guys don't sort stuff out."

James clears his throat. "You're right, and I'll fix this." He looks at Alex. "I'm sorry if I embarrassed you last night. It's the just the thought of you with any other man…"

He doesn't need to finish the sentence. We all get it. I cock my head to the side, gesturing at my cousins. We need to give them privacy to discuss it. Discreetly, we exit the kitchen one by one.

♥♥♥♥♥♥

Ky is using the SatNav to guide him on the drive to my grandparents' house while I bounce in my seat, awash with nerves. "Babe. It's going to be fine. They'll love you."

I give him a frail smile. "I was already nervous about today, but after last night, I'm a million times more nervous." I didn't get to talk to my dad, and I'm wondering how awkward things are going to be between us. I'm also half-expecting a lecture on not following through on my promise to look after Whitney. *Is it wrong that I'm hoping my dad was too drunk and too ashamed to notice the state of his other daughter?*

Ky veers into a short driveway filled with gravel, parking the car in front of a large cream-colored bungalow. The front garden is pretty and colorful and clearly lovingly maintained. The bungalow is an older type of property, but the wide windows look modern, and it seems freshly painted. I wipe my clammy palms down the front of my knee-length white cotton summer dress, opening the door before I can chicken out. Ky rounds the front of the car, pulling me to him. "You've got this, babe, and I have your back." He pecks my lips briefly, and some of my unease lifts. "And you look gorgeous. If anything, you'll dazzle them with your good looks."

I palm my forehead, smiling despite my nerves. "Oh, God help us if you're borrowing cheesy one-liners from Kent now."

He kisses the tip of my nose. "I don't care. I made you smile and think about something else for a minute."

I lean up and kiss him on the lips. "Thanks for coming with me." I take his hand, and we walk toward the front door. Flower boxes adorn each windowsill, and two large hanging baskets decorate either side of the door. They swish in the gentle breeze, and a delicate floral scent wafts through the air. A huge copper pot is packed full of luscious blooms, and I can already tell at least one of my grandparents is into gardening.

The door swings open before I've had time to knock. My dad is framed in the doorway, an anxious expression on his face. "Hi, sweetheart. Can I have a word before I introduce you?"

"Sure." I shuffle uncomfortably on my feet.

Ky hangs back, but Adam shakes his head. "I'd like you to hear this too, Kyler."

Ky lines up behind me, and I rest against his warm body.

Adam looks embarrassed as he speaks. "I'm very sorry about last night. I'm totally ashamed of my behavior. I'd like to blame it on too much whiskey, but that's only partly the reason. I think you know things have been fraught with me and your uncle, and it was only a matter of time before it blew up, but I want you to know that I'm going to fix things. The last thing I want is any tension or awkward feelings because I know how much that would upset you."

"Thank you. I would really love it if you two could find some way of getting on. The past is in the past, and we need to move forward."

He nods, before turning his attention on Ky. "I want you to know I have the utmost respect for your mother. She's a fine lady, and I was way out of line last night. I intend on apologizing to her as soon as I see her. In fact"—his gaze dances between us—"if it's okay with you both, my parents would like to invite the rest of your family over here for dinner later. I told them I would ask you first."

I glance at Ky, and he shrugs, letting me know it's my decision. "I'd like that. If you're sure it's wise?" Perhaps some distance is needed for everyone to cool down.

"I'd rather not let things fester. Best to tackle this head on, if Alex and James are in agreement. I can ring them or—"

"It's okay. I'll call my mom," Ky agrees, removing his phone from his pocket. He steps back a little to make the call.

"I am truly sorry, Faye. Trying to kiss your aunt and fighting with your uncle is something that shouldn't have happened."

"It's okay... Dad. Forget it." *Please drop it.* This is right up there on the never-want-to- think-about-this-type-of-gross-stuff-ever-again scale of awkwardness. I just want to be done with this conversation before it scars me for life.

"They'll be here about six." Ky takes my hand.

"Perfect." My dad loops his arm in mine, and together we step into the house.

My knees are knocking and my heart is thundering in my chest as we walk toward the back of the house. Everyone is waiting outside, apparently. Peals of laughter ring out as we step through a large, comfortable country-style kitchen onto a wide gray-stone patio. I cling to Ky's hand, urging him not to let go. "Breathe, baby," he whispers, sending me a reassuring smile.

A slim blonde-haired woman with a bright smile steps forward to greet us. She is wearing white three-quarter-length trousers and a purple tank top under a flimsy white cardigan. Open-toed sandals adorn her tiny feet. Her nails are painted a vibrant purple. My lip trembles as she gets nearer. A tall distinguished man with salt and pepper hair is playing football with the twins at the side of the large garden. He's obviously my grandfather. Lifting his head up, he smiles. Tousling my brothers' hair, he ambles toward us with an easy gait.

Adam gently tucks me into his side, and I reluctantly let go of Ky's hand. "Mum." Adam beams as the woman stops in front of us. "This is Faye." His adoring gaze brings color to my cheeks. "Faye, this is your grandmother."

I clear my throat. "Hi. It's very nice to meet you, Grandmother." I'm embarrassed that my voice comes out stiff and nervous sounding.

"Call me Eileen, darling. Or Nanna like the other grandkids. Whatever you feel most comfortable with."

"Okay," I squeak, and I'm actually cringing at my own behavior.

She takes my hand in hers as my grandfather steps up. "You're every bit as lovely as Adam told us you were. We've been on a countdown to this day from the moment he told us about you. Especially after our last phone call, haven't we, darling?" She turns to her husband, smiling expansively.

He chuckles. "She's driven all of us demented waiting for this day." He leans in, kissing my cheek, and my skin heats up. He chuckles again. "Don't be nervous. We don't bite." He winks, and the beginnings of a smile lift the corners of my mouth.

My grandmother slaps him playfully on the arm. "Richard. Cut that out. Let the girl settle in before you subject her to your personal brand of humor." She smiles at me. "He has a limited repertoire, so don't expect much and you won't be too disappointed."

Adam groans. "Enough of the comedy act, please."

"And who is this handsome young man?" Eileen asks, extending her hand to Ky.

"This is my boyfriend."

"I'm Kyler Kennedy, ma'am." He takes her hand, placing a gentle kiss on the back of her hand.

"Oh, my." She fans her face with her hand. "Oh, to be young and in love again." Her eyes twinkle as she grins at me. "If you ever grow tired of him, be sure to let me know. I've always wanted to be one of those cougars."

"Jesus, Mum!" Adam's cheeks redden, and it's funny to see him embarrassed over his mother's behavior.

Ky is struggling to contain his mirth, and I grin at him. For the first time, I start to relax. I lean into him. "I'm sorry to disappoint you, Eileen, but he's a keeper."

"Well, darn. There go all my sexy plans."

Adam splutters, and my grandfather laughs, and I can't contain my grin any longer. My grandparents are not at all what I was expecting. They are much younger in appearance and outlook than I imagined, which shouldn't really be that surprising as Dad already told me they were only in their sixties, having raised their family at a young age.

"I hope you're hungry," Richard says. "Eileen cooked enough food for an army." He offers me his arm, and I loop mine in his. "We are going to eat outside if that's okay?"

"Sounds great. And don't worry about any food going to waste. Once my cousins arrive, they will demolish everything in sight."

He chuckles again. "We can't wait to meet them."

We spend a pleasant afternoon outside with my grandparents, chatting, eating, drinking, and laughing. The twins play football until they're ready to collapse. Whitney has been uncharacteristically quiet, picking at her food, and sighing every so often. Adam sends concerned glances her way all afternoon, and it's obvious he's still worried about her. He hasn't said anything about what we got up to last night, so I think we got away with it.

Richard, or Granddad as he's insisting I call him, stokes up the barbecue about an hour before the Kennedys are due to arrive. I help my grandmother clear the table and reset it. We chat about everything and anything as we load dishes into the dishwasher. It's as if they've been a part of my life forever, and I can't believe I was so apprehensive about meeting them. They're two of the loveliest people I've ever met. When I spot Whitney lurking in the corridor, I excuse myself and go to talk to her.

"How's the head?" I joke.

She rewards me with a sour face, and I wonder if all the progress we made last night has already been brushed aside.

"Fine. I can handle my drink, you know." She pouts, thrusting her hip out in an argumentative stance.

"Wasn't implying you couldn't. Did Dad say anything to you?"

"Nope. Not that I was expecting him to. I might as well be invisible."

"That's not true. He's worried about you."

She harrumphs. "Yeah. I'm sure he is."

I frown a little. "You think he doesn't care about you?"

She shrugs. "I don't care either way, and I'm not doing this with you. Just because we shared a moment last night doesn't mean we've automatically turned into the Kardashians."

I pray to God for patience. "I wouldn't want us to be. Look, I'm here for you, and I'll let you call the shots. You have my number. Use it if you need to."

She shrugs again, and I head back outside, frustrated and a little upset if I'm honest. I thought we had turned a corner but it seems we've taken ten steps back.

The gang arrives promptly at six, sans Keven. Alex makes excuses on his behalf, presenting my grandmother with wine, flowers, and a luscious strawberry pavlova. James and Adam stand as far away from one another as possible, doing their best to pretend as if nothing's wrong. Alex is making the introductions, and my cousins are all laying the charm on real thick. "I hope I remember all your names," my grandmother says with a laugh.

"You can blame this lady right here if you can't," Kent supplies, gesturing at Alex. "It was her idea to give us K names. It fit with her brand, isn't that right, Mom."

Alex fails to hide the hurt look on her face, and a potent urge to slap the shit out of Kent accosts me. Ky and Kaden obviously share my sentiment, glaring at Kent and willing him to shut the hell up.

"Actually, that's not technically true," Alex says, recovering quickly. "I had named Kaden and Keven before I even met your father. I liked the idea of calling my children names starting with the same initial, and when I became a Kennedy it made more sense to me to continue the pattern." She smiles at Richard, graciously accepting the glass of sparkling wine he offers her. "If you hate your name so much, Kent, you can petition to have it legally changed." She smiles sweetly at him, taking a small sip of her wine.

Nicely played, Alex. That's one way of putting him in his place.

Chapter Thirteen

Kyler

We say our goodbyes just after nine, and it warms my heart to see Faye pulled into a hug by both her grandparents. I know she was worried about today, and I'm so happy things went well for her. Her grandparents are awesome, and they have welcomed her with open arms.

I'm surprised when Dad tells us to go home without him since he is going for a drink at the local pub with Adam. Mom eyes him warily, but she doesn't protest or warn him not to start any more fights. I'd love to be a fly on the wall for that conversation.

Faye and I watch a couple hours of TV with some of my brothers when we get back to the house before retreating to our room, craving some alone time after spending the entire day surrounded by family. We sit out on the balcony. I'm sipping a soda while Faye is drinking a sparkling water. I pull her feet into my lap, kneading them. "I think today went well."

Her eyes sparkle. "Me too. They're just so… nice and so normal, and I don't feel like an outsider."

"I'm happy for you, babe." I lean over and kiss her sweetly.

"I think I'll have to watch Eileen around you. I definitely caught her ogling you on more than one occasion," she teases.

"What can I say? She's got good taste, like her granddaughter."

Faye laughs, throwing back her head, and her hair swishes over her shoulder. She has the bare minimum of makeup on, and her dress today was simple but elegant. Her beauty is effortless, radiating from the goodness inside her. Every day I fall more and more in love with her.

"What?" she says, studying me curiously.

"I was just thinking how gorgeous you are, inside and out, without even trying. And how lucky I am to have you in my life."

Moisture pools in her eyes. "God, Ky. You are the sweetest, most romantic man I've ever met. I'm the lucky one."

"Sweet? Huh?" My hands wander up her leg, creeping under her dress.

"Hot and sexy too. You're the complete package, babe, and you know it."

"I could say all those things about you too."

She sticks her fingers in her mouth, pretend gagging. "You do realize there's no hope for us now, Ky? We are officially one of those lovey-dovey mushy couples that everyone can't stand."

I lift her up, pulling her into my lap. "I honestly couldn't care less. You are everything to me, Faye, and that is all that matters."

My phone vibrates in my pocket, and I pull it out, cursing the timing. It's Dad. I'm hoping he's not calling to tell me he's flattened Faye's dad to the ground. "Hey."

"Kyler. Could you come and collect me? There are no taxis to be had out this direction, and both Kaden and Keven have been drinking."

He gives me directions, and I hang up promising to be there as quick as I can. Faye already has her shoes on, having overheard most of the conversation. "I'll come keep you company."

Taking her hand, I lead her outside.

We arrive in the small town close to Faye's grandparents' house about twenty minutes later. There are three bars, a convenience store, a vegetable shop, a pharmacy, a butcher, and a gas station, and that's about the extent of it. The streets are clean and empty as I pull up in front of one of the bars. Dad and Adam are leaning against the wall outside, slugging from bottles of beer, with their arms around one another, and they're *singing*. Faye's puzzled expression matches my own.

We climb out of the car, and I round the front, taking Faye's hand. It's as natural to me as breathing these days. We stroll toward our inebriated fathers. They are belting out a U2 classic at the top of their voices, and it's a wonder no one has complained.

"Eh, Dad," Faye says, rubbing the back of her head. "What are you doing?"

"Fixing things," he says, slightly slurring his words.

"How much have you two had to drink?" I pin Dad with a serious expression, and the irony of the role reversal hasn't gone unnoticed.

"Enough," Dad says, stopping singing just long enough to answer me.

"All righty, then," Faye says, looking to me for direction. I just shrug, trying to hide my laughter as Dad attempts to mimic Bono.

"Faye." Adam pushes to his feet, setting his beer on the window ledge behind him. He pulls her into a hug, and I reluctantly let go of her hand. "You don't have to worry anymore. James and I have sorted everything."

"We're good," Dad says, reaching out a hand. I help him stand up.

"I'm glad." Faye looks up at her dad.

He brushes hair back off her face, peering into her eyes with so much adoration. "I have many reasons to be grateful for the life I lead, but never more so than having you in it. I hate that we missed those early years, but I'm so happy we found each other. You are so special to me, sweetheart. And don't think this is drunken babbling because I'm completely sober in this moment. I just need you to know this, honey." Tears glisten in his eyes, and the look of love is unmistakable. "I love you, Faye. So, so much."

A choked sob rips from Faye's throat, and her arms tighten around his waist. "I love you too, Dad," she whispers.

Dad and I walk over to the car, affording them some privacy. They talk in hushed voices, and tears fall silently down Faye's face.

"Is everything really fixed?" I ask Dad while we wait.

He nods. "Life is too short to hold onto grudges or to hate someone for something that happened so long ago. We both acknowledged that."

Dad wraps his arm around my shoulder. "I'm very proud of you, son. I don't think I've told you that enough."

"I know." My muscles stiffen. I can spout romantic endearments to Faye to my heart's content, but emotional conversations break me out in hives.

He chuckles. "I'm very pleased that things are going so well with you and Faye. She's a wonderful girl."

"She is, and I meant every word of what I said that day in the hospital. I *am* going to marry her one day."

"I know, son, and you have our blessing. I know Adam approves too."

"What are you two talking about?" Faye asks with an inquisitive expression.

"Nothing," we both reply at the same time, sharing a conspiratorial smile.

Faye eyes me curiously. "Well, then, let's get these drunken men home to their beds."

♥♥♥♥♥♥

The rest of the week flies by. Faye goes shopping with Whitney, Eileen, and Mom one afternoon while I play a round of golf with Dad, Kal, Kaden, and Keaton. Kade and Kev are still barely speaking to one another, and it would be tense if we weren't so busy all the time. We spend another afternoon with Faye's extended family. Eileen threw a massive barbecue and invited her other children, their spouses, and grandchildren. I think Faye's a little overwhelmed by it all but pleasantly so. Whitney and Kent were caught by Adam making out in the kitchen, and he was not a happy camper, but he didn't make a scene. I caught him and Dad huddled in deep conversation a little while later, and I don't need a crystal ball to work out who or what they were discussing.

Faye is sad saying goodbye to her grandparents on Saturday morning, promising to return for a visit as soon as possible. I'm not sure when we'll find the time once we start college, but I'll move heaven and earth to make it happen if that's what she wants.

Adam, Whitney, and the boys are on the same flight as us, so we rent a minibus to take us to Dublin Airport. Rachel, Sam, and Jill are waiting in the departures lounge, and we have a quick coffee with them before our flight is called. Rachel is sobbing in Faye's shoulder, and my girlfriend is struggling to keep her composure. They part with fervent promises to visit more often.

"Are you okay?" I ask when we are buckled into our first-class seats on the plane.

"Yeah." She looks wistful as she stares out the window. "I had the best time ever, and I'm sad to be leaving my friends, and my new family, but I'm also excited for Harvard, and it feels good to be heading home."

My heart swells with pride and happiness. "It really feels like home?"

She turns to face me with a blinding smile on her face. Raising our conjoined hands to her mouth, she presses a delicate kiss to my skin. "It does."

"Isn't it strange how life can do a complete one-eighty? How everything you thought you knew can change almost overnight." I could say the same for myself.

She nods. "It is. The last time I was on a plane heading to the States, I was in limbo, grieving and unhappy, and I didn't know where my life was headed. It's amazing the difference a year can make."

"I'm glad you're happy. Your happiness is important to me."

She cups my face. "As yours is to me, but you never have to worry about that." She plants a feather-soft kiss on my mouth, and I sigh contentedly. This, right here. This is all I need.

When she pulls back, her eyes are full of happy tears. "As long as you are in my life, I'll always be happy, and I'll always know where home is, because it's wherever you are."

"Ditto, baby. You are my life, and I'm going to spend the entirety of mine making sure you know it."

THE END

♥♥♥♥♥♥♥

Please continue reading, as I've enclosed some bonus content from the series at the back of this book. You can read additional scenes from *Finding Kyler*, bonus scenes in several of the boys' narratives from *Losing Kyler*, and a sample of *Loving Kalvin* and *Saving Brad*, both available to download in e-book, paperback, and audiobook format now.

Bonus Content From Finding Kyler

In this scene, James has just discovered Saoirse has died and learned he has a niece he never knew about. This scene is told from Kyler's perspective.

♥♥♥♥♥♥♥

The cell phone slips out of Dad's hands, crashing to the ground and shattering into a million pieces. Shards of glass litter the tiled floor. Everyone stops talking, looking at him with the same "what the fuck" expressions. Mom rises from the table, hurriedly walking toward him. Dad is visibly trembling, and huge tears tumble silently down his face. My insides tense up as I watch him fall apart.

"What the fuck is going on?" Kal asks in a low tone as I watch my parents for any tell-tale sign. I shrug. Dad latches onto Mom, clinging to her as if he's drowning. She's struggling to prop him up, almost collapsing under his bodyweight.

I walk over to help her. She's trying to get him to look at her, to talk to her, but he's just hanging onto her body, sobbing desperately into her neck.

There's little love lost between Dad and me these days, but it's still hard to see him like this. "What's going on, Mom?" I ask, stepping behind her. I place my arm around her waist to help steady her.

"I'm not sure, Kyler. He's not making much sense."

"Saoirse," Dad mumbles in between sobs, and I frown. *Where have I heard that name before?* And then it hits me. Dad never mentions his long-lost sister in Ireland, and Mom has always told us not to ask after her. They haven't spoken in years, and all I know is that it wasn't Dad's choice to sever ties. Apparently, she decided she wanted nothing to do with him. It's not a topic I've ever given much thought to. She's never been a part of our lives, so I've come to accept that she doesn't even exist. I never give her a second thought. If Dad is crying out her name, it can only mean bad news.

"James." Mom is trying to pry Dad off her, so I reach out and grip his shoulders, helping to pull him upright. Dad grabs me around the shoulders, leaning into me, using me as his new crutch.

This is not who we are.

Awkward doesn't even begin to call it.

The triplets stare open-mouthed at the scene, while a familiar mocking smile is creeping across Kal's mouth. I send him a warning scowl.

"James, please. Just tell me what's wrong. You're scaring us." Mom's eyes crinkle with worry.

That seems to do the trick. He looks over at my brothers, seated quietly around the kitchen table, before his eyes dart to Mom and then me. "Son." He presses his forehead to mine, and I stand there like a dummy, not knowing what to do, how to comfort him, or if I even should.

I clear my throat. "Dad, just let us know what's happened. What is it?"

Smoothing a hand over his hair, he takes a step back, straightening his spine. "I'm sorry, everyone. I've just heard some bad news." Tears well up in his eyes again, and it's like looking at a stranger. I've never ever seen him cry, and I don't like it. Though we haven't gotten on for quite some time, I know I can count on him. It's always there in the background—the knowledge that I can call on him if I need him. No matter how harshly I yell at him, how hard I push him away, I never doubt that he's solid, that's he's always there for me. Except for...

I stop that line of thought before it derails me.

But seeing him like this? Broken? Crying? Like a shell of himself?

It scares me.

He seems so human.

So vulnerable.

Like he isn't invincible and there may come a time when he can't be there for me. When the roles are reversed, and I'll be the one that has to prop him up.

It's unnerving, and I don't like how it's making me feel. I shuffle awkwardly on my feet, shoving my hands into the pockets of my jeans for want of something to do.

"That was Dan," Dad says, referencing my parent's attorney. "He received contact from an Irish attorney, today. My sister and her husband were killed in a car accident five days ago." He swipes under his eyes, and a terrible sadness ages him.

"Oh, James." Mom pulls him into a hug. "I'm so, so sorry."

He shakes his head. "I can't believe it. I always thought there'd be time to repair our relationship. Time to reconnect. Now it's too late."

A strangled sound rips out of his throat, and over at the table, Keaton looks like he's about to bawl. Getting up, he strides toward Dad, wrapping his arms around him without hesitation. "I'm so sorry, Dad. That's awful."

Dad hangs onto Keaton, hugging him to death. A spark of jealousy flares inside me, and I hate myself. It's wrong to resent my brother for having a genuine bond with Dad. Keaton exemplifies the very best of our family. Somehow, he manages to avoid the dark forces plaguing the rest of us.

Mom smiles warmly at them, despite the circumstances, and I know it pleases her that at least one of her sons has a semi-normal relationship with him. Dad shucks out of Keaton's embrace, slapping him affectionately on the back. "There's more." His eyes brighten a little as he scans the room. "She has a daughter. I have a niece."

"What?" Kal asks, his eyes out on stalks. "We have a cousin?"

"Yes. It appears so." He grabs his keys off the counter. "I need to see Dan. There's some paperwork to sort out, and I need to make plans."

"Wait, James." Mom grips his arm to stall him. "I don't understand. What are you saying?"

"Saoirse listed me as her daughter's guardian. I'm going to Ireland to meet my niece, and then she'll be coming to live with us."

Mom went with Dad to the attorney's office, and the rest of us are pretending to watch TV when all everyone is thinking about is our new cousin. "I hope she's hot," Kal pipes up, and I swat him across the back of the head.

"You have such a one-track mind, and you can't perv over her, asshole. She's our cousin."

"I know that, jerk face, but it'd be nice to have something pleasant to look at for a change around here. Besides, she's going to be one of us, and she needs to look the part."

"Now you sound like Mom," Kent snipes.

"Oh, God, Mom is going to treat her like her own personal Barbie doll," Keanu adds with a roll of his eyes.

"Hundred bucks she asks her to model within two minutes of being here," Kal throws out.

I snort. "Only an idiot would take that bet." Mom is legendary for it.

The front door slams shut, and we all perk up. Mom and Dad stroll into the sitting room looking way more animated than when they left. Kaden and Keven trail in their wake, wearing their usual sullen expressions. Kal and I exchange wary looks.

"Good, you're all here," Mom exclaims, taking Dad's hand and pulling him down on the leather couch alongside us. "We want to tell you about Faye."

Mom is practically bubbling with enthusiasm, the kind we rarely see anymore. My sense of trepidation rises a few notches. "She is indeed your father's niece, your cousin, and she's going to be living with us at least until she is eighteen."

"How old is she?" Kal asks.

"Seventeen," Dad replies, and every head swivels in my direction.

"What?" I send them my best "fuck off" face. "She's the same age as me, big fucking deal."

"Kyler." Dad's tone is sharp. "Don't start. My sister just died and I've already missed the funeral, so please, for once, can you stay quiet unless you have anything substantive to add to the conversation."

The asshole is back.

That didn't take long.

I glare at him but keep my mouth closed. I can never say the right thing around him, and I know I'm a big disappointment. The usual anger simmers in my veins and it takes considerable effort to stay tuned into the conversation. The urge to get on the bike and hit the open road is riding me hard.

"We are going to enroll her in O.C., and she'll be a senior, same as Ky. Technically the guardianship is only until she's eighteen, but when January rolls around, we are naturally hoping that she'll remain here with us. She doesn't have any other family. Her father was an only child, and his parents died a few years ago. We are all she has in the world."

Mom laces her fingers in Dad's, and I stare at the unfamiliar sight. I can't remember the last time they were openly affectionate with one another. "She has only just found out about us, too."

"Why all the secrecy?" I ask. We didn't know about her, and she didn't know about us. That's hardly normal. Then again, there is little about the Kennedys that is. Abnormal *is* our normal.

"I don't know," Dad says, but I notice how he can't meet my eyes.

He's hiding something.

"Dad is taking the jet to Ireland the day after tomorrow. They should be back by nightfall. I expect all of you to be here and to be very welcoming. Faye's just lost her parents and found all this out. This will be a huge change for her. Let's help her settle in, and give her whatever support we can." Mom is positively glowing. "I'm taking tomorrow off work to turn one of the guest rooms into a suitable bedroom for her."

Kent turns his head away, but not before I notice the hurtful look on his face. I honestly cannot remember the last time Mom took time off work just like that.

"What's in the file?" Kal asks, gesturing toward the brown paper folder resting on Dad's lap.

"Official documentation, school records, and other stuff."

"Do you have a picture of her?" Kal asks, leaning forward on his knees, excitement written all over his face.

"Yes." Mom extracts a large white envelope from the folder. She hands Kal a bunch of photos, and my brothers all crowd around.

"Damn, she *is* hot!" Kal exclaims, passing the photos around. I stand back, lounging against the arm of the couch, feigning disinterest.

"Kalvin Edward Kennedy." Dad's voice is fierce. "There will be none of that talk around Faye. And, just so I'm clear, she is off limits. She is your cousin, and I don't want any of you laying a hand on her."

"Dad," Keanu cuts in. "Don't be gross."

"She's a pretty girl and hormones are running rampant in this house"—he eyeballs Kal and me in particular, which is ironic because Kent is the one he should really be keeping an eye on—"and this needs to be spelled out." I smirk, folding my arms across my chest. "I mean it, Kyler. Do not touch her." I glare at him, annoyed to be singled out. Kal snickers, and Dad turns his laser-sharp focus on him. "Same goes for you. Grabby hands off her."

I don't understand why he's making such a big deal of this. She's our cousin. There is no need to spell anything out. *Who in their right mind would ever consider going there? Ugh.* A shiver crawls up my spine at the thought.

As if.

♥♥♥♥♥♥

This is the scene leading up to Faye's arrival at the Wellesley house. Also narrated from Kyler's perspective.

I throw my cell down on my bed, groaning. Addison is up to her old tricks, and I'd like to know why. That's the fifth time she's called me this week. I haven't picked up or called her back *or* responded to the twenty texts she's sent me. But I know her. When she gets something into her head, she throws her all at it. *No* isn't in her vocabulary.

Maybe that's why she ended up fucking my best friend, who I've been told was chasing after her behind my back for months. You think you know someone, when really you don't have a clue who they are. I shake my head, still pissed after all this time.

But I miss the disloyal prick, and I hate myself for that.

Frustrated, I head to the gym and work up a sweat. My thoughts flit to my new cousin who is on her way here right now. Dad is late and Kaden has been frothing at the mouth over missing study time.

I snort. As if I'm buying that.

Foregoing pussy time, more like. I can tell there's someone new on the scene. Not that he'd tell you anything. He's the cagiest of all of us.

After I've showered and changed, I head down to the garage to check the documentation is in order. Rick has organized storage for the bikes at the warehouse, and transportation is arranged for tomorrow. I want to make sure my babies have a smooth ride. The sound of voices reaches me as I step into the garage. I falter, every hair standing to attention on my body.

Slim, jean-clad legs swing out the side of the car, and I step back, keeping firmly in the shadows as I catch the first glimpse of my cousin. Her black-and-white Converse bounce off the ground as she straightens up, her thick garishly red locks swaying from side to side. She walks briskly toward my bikes, and my eyes rake up and down her long legs. Her clingy black sweater hugs curves that are all woman, and her shapely ass molds to her form-fitting jeans. Blood rushes to my dick, and I frown, never taking my eyes off her. Dad is chatting to Max in the corner, oblivious to my presence.

Her fingers coast over my bike, sweeping lovingly over the bodywork and dipping into the grooves in the tires. My eyes lock on her fingers, watching every caress with an intensity bordering on craving, and I wonder what her hands would feel like touching my body. She bends slightly at the waist, her fingers tracing a line farther down the tires, her hair falling in cascading waves over her shoulder. I've a sudden urge to run my fingers through it, to bury my head in the strands, to see if she smells as good as she looks.

I jerk back, almost tripping over a box at my feet. Things are getting tight in my jeans, and I scrub a hand over my prickly jaw, as my heart starts pounding furiously in my chest. I'm totally shocked at my reaction, and instant self-loathing travels up my throat. I should feel grossed out, but instead, I'm turned on. I'm a fucking pervert, hiding in the shadows, checking out my cousin's ass.

Without giving it another thought, I cross the space, heading straight for her. She's still engrossed in the bike, and she only registers my approach at the last second. "Get your hands off my bike," I snap in the harsh tone I usually reserve for my father.

As she straightens up, a faint red blush appears on her chest, rising to her neck. Her head is down, and she's not meeting my eyes, but I watch as her gaze treks from my feet and up my legs, before zoning in on my abs. Her tongue darts out, and she licks her lips. Slightly parted, her lips are full and inviting, and the urge to suck and bite on her lower lip is almost overwhelming. But I'm a master at disguise, and no hint of what I'm feeling will ever be displayed on my face.

She tilts her chin up as she continues her exploratory journey beyond my chest and onto my face. Mesmerizing, wide, blue eyes, framed within a set of long, thick, dark lashes meet mine, and instant desire ties my insides into knots.

Dad should be shot for calling her merely 'pretty.'

She's way more than that.

Her skin looks pale against the brash red hair, but it's smooth and clear except for the smattering of tiny freckles across her nose and the faint stain on her cheeks. Her V-neck sweater doesn't quite conceal all she's got going on, and I can detect the swell of her generous breasts just peeking out from under the edge of a lace-trimmed vest.

My dick is rock-hard in my jeans, and I'm hoping she doesn't notice.

Fuck me.

She's been sent here as a test.

There can be no other reason why the first girl I'm attracted to *in months* just happens to be my cousin—a girl I'm forced to live with day in, day out—*and* there's a strict "hands off" policy in place. Not that Dad's warning would stop me if I wanted to take it there.

How the hell am I going to resist a taste when I'm already primed to explode and she's just set foot in the door?

My dick twitches in my pants, and I know I'm totally fucking screwed.

No wonder Dad warned me off her.

Bringing a girl like Faye into our house is akin to inviting Hugh Heffner around to party twenty-four-seven.

What's worse is I see the way she's looking at me, the way her body is subtly reacting to mine, and I know she's feeling the chemistry too.

What an absolute nightmare.

I've been staring at her with indifference, but now it's time to put my real game face on. This can't happen, and it's time to make that abundantly clear. Crossing my arms over my chest, I glare at her, trying to ground myself.

This shit can't happen. Not ever.

Snarling, I pin her with my most lethal look. "Are you done drooling yet?"

Her eyes narrow to slits as a smirk spreads over her mouth. "Don't flatter yourself. You're the first specimen of prime American a-hole I've seen. I wanted to memorize the form so I know what to avoid the next time."

Kill. Me. Now.

Although her tone is biting, the smooth, husky quality to her voice contrasts perfectly with her lilting Irish accent, and I'm done for. Combine that with her gorgeousness and her obvious sass, and this is a lost cause. Nonetheless, I've a part to play, so I smirk back at her, acting as if her words just glided over my head instead of super-charging my arousal. I spot the flare of anger in her eyes before she schools her features into an impressively blank façade.

Her fingers twitch as she continues to feign indifference. Her reaction is like a shot of liquid lust straight to my crotch. I force my smirk higher, almost laughing when a sneer washes over her face. This is going to be a living hell, and I need to deflect it now, so I lean down close to her ear, ignoring the compelling urge to pull her body flush against mine, and attempt to warn her off. "I don't know how they do things in Ireland, sweetheart, but you're in my house—in my domain. And you don't get to talk shit to me. Keep out of my way, and I'll keep out of yours. Same goes for my brothers."

If I'm having this reaction, I can only imagine how Kal is going to respond. He can barely keep it in his pants as it is. If he even looks funny at her, I swear I'll...

You'll what? I ask myself.

Shit, now I'm getting territorial.

As if she's mine.

In a different lifetime, I can already see that. How easy it would be to fall for her. To want to keep her. To make her mine.

My thoughts scare the shit out of me.

What the hell is happening to me?

If she were just any girl, I'd probably be rejoicing right now. Because I've thought for so long that I'd never be able to feel anything for any girl again. To ever risk letting anyone in. Not after my heart was smashed into pieces. But as I look at this girl, this stranger, who I've known for all of five seconds, I know I could do it with her. She could be that for me.

If only she wasn't my cousin.

END OF BONUS SCENE

Bonus Content From Losing Kyler

This is the scene from Chapter 20 of Losing Kyler where Brad takes Faye back to the lake to help distract her from the impending test results. These scenes are narrated from Brad's perspective.

♥♥♥♥♥♥♥

"I love it here," I say, pausing to drink my soup. My limbs are stiff with the bitter cold, and I must be crazy to have brought Faye out here today. Even though the thick plaid blanket is draped over her lower half, she's visibly shivering. I'm a thoughtless ass. "I've spent a lot of time here the last few months. It's one of the few places where I can organize my thoughts into some kind of order."

It's true. Out here, with only the wildlife for company—and the odd grumpy fisherman—I can calm the cluttered thoughts in my mind. The sensation is fleeting. The minute I step back into normalcy, all the usual worries return. But out here, I can find some inner peace.

"Is that why you brought me here?" she asks.

Yes. And no.

I look directly into her wide, trusting blue eyes. "I know you've got to be worried. You get the results on Monday, but you haven't said one word to me since the last time we were here. I thought you might need an ear to bend."

I *am* concerned for her. She's had to deal with so much these last few months. Deal with much worse crap than me, and she's been restless all week. I know she's freaking out over the test results, and I figured it would do her good to get out of the house.

But that's only half the truth.

I wanted to get her alone. *Needed* to get her alone. I crave her company like a kid craves cotton candy at a fair. All this fake boyfriend shit is totally fucking with my head. There's nothing fake about it on my part, and I'm not sure how much longer I can continue to deny my feelings.

The more I get to know her, the more I want to.

And I don't just mean as her friend.

She groans, and that little noise she makes at the back of her throat is exquisite.

"Why'd you have to be so bloody perfect?" she asks, and damn, if that doesn't warm up all the frozen parts of me.

I'm far from perfect, but who am I to shatter a girl's illusions? She's edging dangerously close to where I'd like to bring this convo. Even though I know there's a strong possibility this won't go the way I want it to go, I refuse to pass up the opportunity. Shoot me if that makes me selfish. I've spent weeks acting all selfless and saint-like—I believe I've earned my shot. I raise my brows. "Let's imagine, hypothetically, that that's true," I say, lifting my palm when I see her mouth opening to say something. "Why is it a problem?"

Her beautiful face contorts. "It makes it harder."

My brow furrows in confusion. "I don't understand."

She groans again, and I sit on my hands to avoid acting on the impulse to reel her into my arms and kiss the heck out of that sultry mouth. She places her cup on the ground and runs her hands over her face. "Do I have to spell it out?"

The anguish and uncertainty in her gaze is obvious in the extreme, and I take pity on her. I lean in closer, and a dart of electricity zings through my veins when our knees collide. Her touch does the most amazing things to me, and I long to know if it's the same for her. I know she cares about Ky. I'm not an idiot. But I have eyes in my head, and I see the way she looks at me sometimes. The way she reaches for me instinctively without even realizing what she's doing. She feels *something* for me. Whether it's enough is yet to be seen, but I'm done playing it safe. Time to bring it to the next level.

She needs to understand she has options.

Forcing a trace of guilt aside, I take her hands in mine, biting back a wince as her icy-cold skin impacts mine. Dammit! I should've thought to bring gloves for her. I force my lips into a playful smile, figuring it's best to downplay this so I'm less humiliated if it doesn't go my way. "A gentleman never makes the lady go first." Before I can chicken out, I spit the words I've been harboring in my heart out through my mouth. "I'm falling for you, Faye, but you already know that."

She's struggling to hold my gaze, and my heart pounds anxiously in my chest. My eyes penetrate hers, conveying the full extent of my words, my emotions. Although Faye is one of the most beautiful girls I've ever seen, my attraction for her goes way deeper. She's the first girl since Rose who I've made a real connection with. I can be myself around her without fear, and I think it's the same for her. None of the relationships I've had since Rose have ever meant anything or were ever going anywhere because they were too superficial. I couldn't talk to any of those girls the way I can talk to Faye. On a basic level, we understand each other in a way that's so rare. So refreshing.

She's got to realize that too.

"And we'd be so good together, I know we would." My voice resonates with confidence. Confidence I'm struggling to hold onto in light of the conflict playing out on her face.

Fuck. *What have I done?* I've opened a hornet's nest, that's what.

"I know that too," she whispers. "In a lot of ways, we are so alike. We're dealing with similar situations; we both have no parents around, and I know you feel lonely and disconnected like I do. I know we could be good for one another. I know all these things."

And it's still not enough. She doesn't need to say it. I see it written all over her face. "But?" I keep a neutral expression on my face. "I know there's one coming, and I'm fairly sure I know what it is."

She cups my face, and her touch reaches all the way to my toes. I want to kiss her so badly it feels like I might die if my lips can't taste hers.

"You're hot, and sweet, and funny, intelligent, and so thoughtful, and I could list a hundred other ways you are endearing."

Well, that's a brush-off if ever I heard one. My heart sinks.

She presses her forehead to mine. "I wish I was falling for you, too. I wish that more than anything, but I can't force myself to feel a certain way," she whispers.

Inwardly, I curse myself for my arrogant stupidity. I should've known better than to take things here. I always end up playing second fiddle to Kyler Kennedy, so I don't know why I thought this situation would be any different. Attempting to smother my disappointment, I force those nasty thoughts from my mind. It's only the rejection speaking. Ky's like a brother to me, and that won't ever change. He isn't my competition, even if it might seem that way sometimes.

She eases back, putting some distance between us, and my heart throbs in a familiar way. "I'm sorry, Brad. Maybe, in the future, my feelings will change, but I still love him. I love Ky."

"He's with Addison," I blurt out, foolishly clinging onto the impossible.

"I know that." She kicks out at the gravel underfoot, and her lips pull into a grim line. "Unfortunately, it doesn't help. I know I could be fooling myself, but I still think she's forcing him into it some way."

I've had the same suspicions, but I'm not so sure anymore. That fucking bitch knows how to dig her claws in deep. Faye doesn't understand that. She didn't see them when they were together, before all that shit went down. Ky worshiped the ground Addison walked on, and there was a time when I was majorly jealous of what they shared.

That ship has long since sailed, and I wouldn't wish that malicious tramp on anyone. Least of all someone I care about. Which is why seeing him with her again is so painful. Especially when it appears to be legit. At least, that's what Ky is telling me. If I had a choice between those girls, I wouldn't hesitate to pick the girl in front of me. I wouldn't even need to consider it for a second—Faye is, hands-down, a million times the girl Addison is. But, hey, if Ky wants to be a brain-dead dick, then it's his loss and my potential gain. She's single. I'm single. He can't have anything to say about it. "Faye, I'm not saying this to hurt you, but you've got to open your eyes. You saw them at the party, and I've asked him repeatedly if there's something going on we're not aware of, and he insists there isn't."

Her body locks up, and she rises stiffly, thrusting the full extent of her frustration at me. "And did he tell you that with his real face on or the mask he hides behind?" she snipes. I bend down, idly picking up a stone at my feet, deliberately not responding. In a couple of months, she's managed to see what took me years to discover. "Exactly my point."

I fling the stone out across the lake, wondering, again, why I thought it was such a good idea to bare my heart and soul. As if both weren't already shredded. "If he's your brother, it's a moot point," I tell her, bluntly stating the facts.

She drops down on the log. "I know."

The look of utter despair on her face is like a knife to the throat. I hate that I'm partly responsible for putting it there. I take her hands in mine. "I'm sorry. I know I shouldn't be hitting you with this when you're dealing with something so difficult. I'm just frustrated because I like you and I know you like me and I wish it was enough, but I'm being selfish. I'm sorry."

She squeezes my hands, her look softening. "Don't apologize. There's no need. I feel the same way, and this might not last forever. I don't know how I'm going to feel next week if the tests confirm James is my dad and my cousins are my half-brothers. Instead of using this time to get used to the idea, I've buried my head in the sand, and now I'll have to face the consequences of my actions."

"You're hoping James is wrong."

She nods. "So much, and not purely because of Ky." She averts her eyes, ashamed. "I can't wrap my head around the fact that my mum slept with her brother and that she lied to me about everything that was important. What kind of person does that?"

"I don't know, Faye. I've spent months wondering how my dad could steal from his clients and his friends, querying whether I actually know him at all." The usual pang hits me in the gut.

"Yes!" she says with real feeling. "That's how I feel, too. It's like the person I grew up respecting and admiring and loving was a fraud."

"And it makes you question your own identity and your judgment and the things you value." Man, it's too easy to talk to this girl. I'm pissed at her rejection, but I can't even blame her for that. I love talking with her like this. I can't tell anyone else this stuff—the words get trapped in my throat but not with her. Never with her. I clutch her hands tighter, wishing so much that she was mine. "Or at least it has for me."

She nods eagerly. "Me, too. Even more so because my identity is now entangled with another family's, and it's like I don't belong anywhere."

"I can relate to that, too." I tip her chin up with my finger, ignoring the urge to pull her face to mine. We stare at one another, and that unspoken chemistry sizzles between us. She's got to feel it! It can't just be me.

Her eyes roam my face, settling on my mouth, and her tongue darts out, licking her voluptuous lips. All the blood rushes to my dick. I scan her rose-colored cheeks, the tortured indecision in her eyes, and the patchy reddish flush creeping up her neck. Visions of holding her in my arms that one time, my lips locked with hers, surge to the forefront of my mind. Kissing her was like tasting heaven. As my eyes drop to her mouth, I remember how soft her lush, plump lips felt moving against mine. How absolutely fucking perfect she felt in my arms. How the feel of her body pressing against mine sparked desire so intense I thought I'd come in my pants right then and there. My chest rises as unbridled longing clouds all logical thought. I'm grateful for the blanket, concealing the rock-solid hard-on in my jeans. I peer into her eyes, begging her to give into this. When she moves forward, inching slowly toward me, I can't stop the smile from spreading over my mouth.

This is happening.

I lean closer, and butterflies swamp my chest. Hells, I'm turning into such a pansy around her, but I don't care. She's worth it. Even my relationship with Ky won't hold me back.

She's worth risking everything.

There's barely an inch between us, and I could close that gap in a heartbeat. I want to, but for the glimmer of hesitation in her eyes. She's got to be the one to do it. *She's got to kiss me.*

Because I know her, truly know her, I see it the second she's made her decision. Before she pulls back. Before she confirms it verbally. "I'm sorry, Brad. Can we head back, please? I'm cold."

I'm standing beside her on the pavement, staring at Ky's bike outside the store across the way. "Could be," I lie after she's asked if it's his, "but he's not the only one with that make and model in the town."

We don't talk as we wait in line for coffee, and I'm feeling like more and more of a jackass. I should let this go. I know she's confused, and I'm only making things worse, but I can't. It's selfish, but I can't help myself. I want her too much.

We drink our coffee on the bench outside the café. I clear my throat. "Faye?"

"Hhm." She peers up at me through thick, hooded lashes, with the tip of her nose rosy-red and her cheeks flushed from the cold. Her hair falls in messy tangles over her shoulders, and I've never seen anyone more beautiful. Most of the girls in this town wouldn't be seen dead without a scrap of makeup, let alone hunched up in a puffy, unflattering jacket, with knotty hair and muddy boots. But that only adds to Faye's allure. She's completely unaware of her beauty, and she doesn't try to be something she's not. I noticed that about her from the get-go, and it didn't take long to become obsessed with her. Of course, I didn't realize she had already started something with her cousin, because what normal person would ever contemplate that? By the time I found out, it was too late. I was completely smitten.

I draw a brave breath and ask the question that's ghosted over my lips the entire drive back to Wellesley. "I know you wanted to kiss me back there as much as I wanted it. Why'd you stop?"

"Because it will only make things more complicated," she replies, with transparent honesty.

She didn't say because she didn't want to, and that injects me with a much-needed dose of confidence. Could be delusion. "Or it could have the opposite effect." I snake my arm around her shoulder, and my fingers tease the ends of her hair.

"Maybe." She shrugs, and I silently punch the air. It's not an outright no.

I slide down the bench, brushing my leg against hers as I tip her face up. "If you kiss me, we'll both know either way." Expectation is rife in the air, and I'm holding my breath in anticipation of her reply.

"I don't want to ruin our friendship."

"How about this," I say, reeling her into my arms. Her wide, innocent eyes stare deep into mine, and I'm drowning in the most blissful daze. Rousing myself, I focus on sealing the deal. I can't not kiss her now. I need to kiss her—I'll go insane otherwise. "One kiss. One *meaningful* kiss"—I drag the word out so there can be no confusion over what I'm asking—"no strings attached. If you're feeling it, you agree to go on a date with me and see where it goes. If you don't feel anything, then I'll walk away. I swear I won't bring it up again, and I promise I will not let it affect our friendship." She worries her lip between her teeth, and I can't take my eyes off her. "Your call."

Please say yes. I chant it over and over in my head like I'm demented. If she bails now, I think I'll die.

Her knee jerks up and down, and her brow creases as she mulls it over in her head.

"Jeez, throw a guy a line here." I try to keep my tone lighthearted, but the desperation shines through.

Her arms creep around my neck, and I've stopped breathing altogether. "Okay. One kiss." I open my mouth to speak, but she silences me with one carefully placed finger. Fireworks explode in my gut, and saliva pools in my mouth. "One *meaningful* kiss."

Hells yeah! I suck her finger into my mouth, running my tongue over her silky flesh, grinning like an idiot when she emits a little breathy gasp.

Desire is rampaging through my body. The urge to crush my lips to hers and ram my tongue in her mouth is riding me hard, but she deserves so much more than pure, animalistic monkey lust. Everything rests on this one kiss, and I've got to make it count. Attacking her with the extent of my lust won't help my chances. I need to do this slow and steady. Or as slow and steady as I can manage.

I carefully remove her finger from my mouth and pull her in tight to my chest. My thumb smooths a line around her lips, and I bite back a moan. I move in, kissing just under her ear, ready to throw a frigging party when she trembles discernibly under my touch. I plant light kisses up and down her face from her ear to her jaw to her cheek, back and forth, inhaling the sweet scent of her skin and forcing myself to stay away from the main prize. "Last chance to back out," I whisper, silently cursing myself for giving her a last-minute reprieve.

She closes the gap and presses her lips to mine. I swear, my whole body comes alive. I finally have her where I want her, and it's everything I remember and more. Her kiss is feather-soft, and I sense a little hesitation. It's moved beyond the point where I can let her off the hook. One meaningful kiss means exactly that. Wrapping my arm firmly around her waist, I tilt my head to the side and deepen the kiss, my lips moving solidly over hers. This feels too good to be real. Her warmth, her softness, her sweet allure—it's almost too much, and, yet, nowhere near enough at the same time. I intensify the kiss, growing braver as I battle against my raging hormones. When her fingers drift through my hair, sending lusty tingles all over my body, I can't stifle the moan that escapes my lips.

I crush my mouth to hers, licking the seam of her lips, and she opens for me. Our tongues dart out, tangling deliciously, and the bulge in my boxer briefs strains against my jeans, almost to the point of pain. One touch from Faye returns me to my horny fourteen-year-old body. She moves onto my lap, placing her tempting ass right over my aching cock, and I devour her mouth, pouring everything I feel into it. I can scarcely believe she's kissing me back with the same need. Her fingers fist in my hair, tugging almost painfully on my head, and her hands inch down, trailing over my neck and shoulders, and I shudder underneath her skillful touch.

I don't know how long we kiss for. All I know is I never want it to end.

At some point, we break apart, panting as we both suck in lungsful of air. My lips are slick and swollen, and I'd happily return for a second round. Her head rests on my shoulder, and I strengthen my hold on her, keeping my arms firmly around her waist as I pull her in tight to me.

Her body goes stiff at the angry roar of an engine. I don't look over the road. I don't need to. I sensed he was watching. *Does it make me a shitty friend that I hoped he was watching?* Ky's with Addison now, but he's still possessive of Faye, and he needs to let her go. In a warped way, maybe this will help him make the right decision.

Man, I'm not just a shitty friend. I'm a shitty human. Can't even lie to myself. I'm a worthless piece of crap to have done this to my friend.

I curse at the same time she jumps up, running onto the road with no concern for her safety. I intercept one decidedly hostile look from Ky before he cranks the engine and maneuvers the bike out into the traffic.

I stalk to my car, furious at the entire fucking world. I kick the car into gear the second Faye locks her seatbelt, powering up the road, fueled by anger and self-loathing.

"Slow down or you'll kill us both, please." Her pleading tone and look help take the edge off my anger.

I ease back a little on the pedal, thoughts churning like violent waves in the midst of a raging storm. "Don't tell me you didn't enjoy that because I can tell you did," I say, a muscle pulsing in my jaw. My head is all over the place, and I know I should say nothing, but I've lost the run of myself.

"I'm not going to deny that," she admits, turning to face me.

My fingers dig into the steering wheel, sensing all that she's not saying. I'm awash with hurt and self-regret. "But let me guess. It's still not enough."

She doesn't even attempt to deny it, and I reluctantly admire her honesty. "I'm sorry."

I don't respond because there's nothing left to say. We drive back to the house in uncomfortable silence. I park the car and turn off the engine, and we sit there in silence, neither one of us attempting to make a move.

It's not fair to be mad at her. I instigated this. I pushed her knowing full well how she feels about Ky. I'm the one who brought her full throttle into my delusional little bubble. I wanted to turn fantasy into reality so bad, but all I've done is potentially drive her away. I don't want that. As bad as not being able to touch her is, it would be ten million times worse if I lost her for good. It's up to me to make this right. "Okay. You kept your side of the bargain, and I'll keep mine."

"I hope you mean that because you're important to me." I don't doubt her sincerity because it echoes in her words, and it's who she is.

I know she likes me—just not enough.

I know she needs me—just not in the way I want her to need me.

"You're way too important to cut out of my life. I'll get over it," I lie again, pressing a light kiss on the back of her hands. "Friends?" I almost choke on the word.

She smiles sadly through wary, keen eyes. "Friends."

♥♥♥♥♥♥♥

Ky is keeping a low profile, and I've been doing the same, but nothing will get resolved like that. I'd half-expected him to charge me the second we stepped foot in the house, but he's been gone for hours. Faye could barely look at me during dinner and I hate myself for this tension that's brewing between us. I thought of going to her, to reassure her that everything is cool, but I figure I've lied to her enough today. Time apart is probably the best thing right now.

Which means that I have too much head space, and that's never a good thing anymore. I haven't felt this heartbroken since Rose and I split, although that was a completely different scenario. Things had naturally fizzled out between us, and the decision to break up was mutual and amicable, but it was still difficult. I was only fifteen, but the sadness had been like nothing I'd ever felt before, and I missed her. After a few weeks, I plucked up the courage to contact her, to ask if we could still be friends, and it was one of the best decisions of my life. Rose is one of my best friends, and one of the few people who stuck by me after all that shit with Dad. I often wonder what might have happened if we hadn't dated so young. *If we'd met at another juncture in our lives, would things have worked out differently?*

Damn. I rub my prickly jaw. I've really sunk to a new low if I'm regurgitating those old nostalgic thoughts. What's done is done, and there's no going back. Rose is happy with Theo, and he's good for her. But even if she wasn't with anyone, I know she isn't the one for me. I'm not idiotic enough to think Faye was all that, but in time, she might have been.

Ky and I have always had similar thoughts when it comes to girls. We're both more of a relationship type of guy, although we've had our fair share of hookups and casual dating. But there's no appeal in that anymore; I'm ready for a relationship. A meaningful one. Have been for a while, and Faye is the first girl in a long time to spark any kind of real interest.

Trust me to pick the one girl who is never going to pick me.

Not when she has a choice between me and my best friend.

Ky and I have always been drawn to the same type of girl, and it's caused more arguments than I care to think about over the years. I know I was drunk when Addison pounced, but deep down, I have wondered if there wasn't some subconscious part of me reveling in the fact that she was choosing me over him, even if I had zero interest in her. The irony is that she was one girl we hadn't come to fisticuffs over. Until that happened. Irony is a bitch on steroids.

Dammit. I rub my face. I definitely put the shitty in shitty friend.

It's well after midnight when the quiet hum of Ky's bike approaching the house tickles my eardrums. I pad in my bare feet to the kitchen to wait for him.

We need to thrash this out.

"Unless you want a fist in the face, I suggest you get the fuck out of here" are the first words out of his mouth. He slams his helmet down on the counter, turning his back on me as he strides to the fridge.

"We need to talk."

He pulls the OJ out of the fridge, pops the lid, and chugs straight from the carton. "I have nothing nice to say to you."

I push off the counter and lean against the side of the fridge. "I know you're pissed, but we have to discuss this. We're both living in this house with her, and we can't let this fester."

He throws the empty carton into the sink, turning to glare at me. "Living arrangements can always change."

I shrug. He can threaten all he likes. I know him. He won't kick me out.

Maybe I'll save him the trouble. Perhaps that's the solution. I can ring Aunt Cora and ask to stay with her. Sure, the commute to school will be a bitch, but I'll manage. "If you want me to leave, just say the word, and I'll be gone."

"Don't push me, man, I'm still way too wired." His shoulder bumps mine as he stalks away, flinging his leather jacket over a chair as he storms into the living room.

I trail behind him, determined to get this over and done with now. "Why?" I ask, dropping onto the couch across from him. "You are with Addison. Why do you care?"

A muscle pops in his jaw. "I never said I didn't care about her. She's my... she's my cousin."

I bark out a laugh. "You are fucking pathetic, dude. Do you stand in front of the mirror trying to convince yourself of that shit?" And here I thought I was the delusional one.

"Shut the fuck up." His foot taps furiously up and down, and he's primed to explode.

Maybe the fact I'm still goading him indicates I'm feeling exactly the same. "You have no claim on Faye, on who she dates, who she kisses, so why do you have an issue with her kissing me?" I lean back, locking my hands around my head. "Or is that it? She can kiss anyone as long as it isn't me? Is this some prolonged form of punishment because I fucked Addison while she was your girl?"

He glares at me, his fists clenching at his sides. And I'm a masochist 'cause I keep pushing him. "'Cause I gotta tell you, man, you definitely drew the short straw. Faye is worth a million of Addison, and if you don't want her, I sure as hell do." Steam practically billows out of his ears, and I push it all the way. "I want her. I want Faye so fucking much. Over me, under me, in every way I can get her."

I'm a Class-A jerk masquerading as a good guy. I could've just asked him to hit me. I didn't need to disrespect Faye to do it, but sometimes Ky needs to be pushed to extremes to open himself up.

He totally flips, jumping up and swinging at me with his fists. The first punch is extremely satisfying. So is the second and third one. My head lolls back, and the stinging pain along my jawline distracts from the emptiness in my chest. The fourth punch less so, but I let him have at it.

Unexpectedly, he stops, rearing back and dropping to his butt on the floor.

I rub my sore jaw as my gaze narrows on him, noting the drooped shoulders and the pain flaring across his eyes. He can't hide it any longer, and it's exactly as I suspected. "Just tell me, man. Tell me what Addison is threatening to force you to toe the line."

He looks down at his feet, shaking his head, and I know that's all the affirmation I'm going to get. "At least tell Faye. You're hurting her."

He climbs slowly to his feet, plopping back down on the other couch. "I can't. It's for the best."

I sit up, leaning my elbows on my knees. "No offense, dude, but you make the worst decisions where Addison is concerned."

"And you think I don't know that?!" he yells, looking me directly in the face.

The full extent of his misery is revealed, and a huge surge of guilt waylays me. My gut told me he was being blackmailed into this, but I was happy to push that aside to win the girl. "I'm a shitty friend," I admit.

"You are," he readily agrees. "But I'm an equally shitty one."

"Always turning it into a competition," I joke.

He rolls his eyes, and silence settles in the room.

"I'm sorry I hit you," Ky says a couple of minutes later.

"I probably deserved it," I reply. No probably about it.

"No, you didn't." He pauses momentarily. "And you're right. I have no claim over her. Faye's free to kiss whomever she likes."

He's as bad at lying to himself as I am.

"I swore I'd never do that to you again." And I did.

"You haven't done anything wrong, man. If I'm not with her, I'd rather it be you. I know I can I trust you to look after her, to treat her right."

He knows I'd treat her like a princess. I only wish I had the chance. "It doesn't matter, anyway. She doesn't want me." There's a finality to my tone I hope he detects, because after today, I know there isn't a snowball's chance of a relationship with Faye. Particularly when Ky has all but admitted he's pushed her away to protect her. He only does that for those he loves.

"That wasn't the way it looked to me," Ky says, failing to hide his jealousy.

"She's in love with you." It kills me to say it, but it's the truth.

"She can't be!" he snaps out of frustration. "Hasn't she listened to a word I've said? She needs to move on, and you're the guy to move on with. Do you want me to talk some sense into her?"

Before I can respond, a burst of bright light fills the room, and Faye is charging across the floor with her nostrils flaring. Fuck! *How much of that did she hear?* My eyes widen in surprise as she plows into Ky, pushing him forcefully in the chest. "I do not need anyone to talk sense into me, least of all you!" She's shrieking like a hyena, and I've never seen her so enraged. "How dare you presume to know what I want or what I need. You have no right!"

"Faye." I stand up, hands raised in appeal. She lunges at me, pushing me back down on the couch. It's hot as hell, and I work hard to contain my grin. "And you're no better!" she seethes. "You think you can get his permission and I'll fall into your arms?"

That sobers me up. I don't want her thinking that either of us would ever treat her with such disrespect. "No! It wasn't like that."

"I heard enough to know that he was trying to pawn me off on you." She points in Ky's direction, and her eyes narrow when she notices the dark look he's leveled her with. "Wipe that smug look off your face, Ky, or I'll do it for you." She scowls at him, but it's like a fish baiting a shark. Ky can't stop his grin, and that only infuriates her more. "Do you have a death wish?" she hisses.

He stands up, moving leisurely toward her. "Baby, you know I find it hot when you're mad."

An uneasy feeling creeps up my spine. If this is some form of arguing-slash-making-up, I don't want to stick around to witness it. Faye shoves him, and he loses his balance when he tries to grab her. They both stumble to the floor, and she ends up straddling him in a way that cranks my envy to the max. A sour taste floods my mouth. Ky is devouring her with a lusty gaze, like he wants to strip her naked and take her right here on the floor. She prods his chest, anger mingling with raw need on her face, and I don't have to force myself to look away. The emptiness in my chest is gone. Replaced by a sharp, stabbing pain that makes me feel way too much.

"You don't get to flirt with me, to call me baby, or hot, or anything!" She scrambles to her feet. "Save it for your girlfriend!"

She takes a step back, and I hate to see the frown creasing her brow. "I want nothing to do with either of you. Understood?"

Ky pulls himself upright.

Hell, no. I can't deal with that. I stand up, moving toward her. "Faye, I'm sorry. Come on."

She sways a little on her feet, and we both incline toward her. "Leave me alone, Brad. Both of you. Stay away from me."

Ky and I exchange glances as she stomps to the kitchen, returning a couple of seconds later with a bottle of water in each hand. She ignores us completely as she bolts past us like a fireball.

"Aw, fuck it!" Ky protests, dropping onto the couch with a loud sigh. "Now she's pissed at both of us."

"I don't blame her. We're assholes."

Ky sits upright, shaking his head. "No. *You're* not. You make this right with her. I can't, but you can." His eyes drill into mine. "She needs more protection. I don't trust Addison not to hurt her."

"I won't let anything happen to her." I get to my feet. "I promise. I'll protect her. *We'll* protect her."

Ky nods, and for the first time in ages, we are on the same page.

This is from Chapter 13 of Losing Kyler where Faye and Brad visit Kaden at Harvard. This scene is narrated by Kaden and it shows what happens before he opens the door to his cousin.

♥♥♥♥♥♥

"Mr. Kennedy? Did you hear anything I just said?" Professor Garcia taps her pen impatiently off the top of the desk in my bedroom, her whiskey-colored eyes narrowing as she assesses me under long, thick lashes.

"Huh?" I say rather unintelligibly, finally tearing my gaze from her delicate hands.

"This is a waste of my time." She gathers her books and papers. "I only take on one or two students a year to personally tutor. I'm not inclined to give up my free time for someone who clearly has zero interest and who is ill-prepared to put in the required degree of effort." She stuffs her things in her expensive black leather briefcase and stands up.

That snaps me out of my funk. "I'm sorry. Please don't leave. I am very grateful for this opportunity, and I *am* prepared to work. I promise."

Her eyes bore into mine as she purses her pouty lips in contemplation. "You've barely listened to a word I've said these last twenty minutes, and you can't stop yawning. Either I'm boring you to tears or you pulled an all-nighter." I open my mouth to offer some kind of excuse—because there's no way in hell I'm telling her I'm exhausted from last night's sexcapade with Tiffani—but she holds up a hand, immediately stopping me. "I don't want to know."

My gaze languishes on her beautiful hand, and I'm distracted all over again. I don't know if she's aware, but she gestures with her hands a lot while she's explaining, and I think I've developed a brand new hand fetish. Her long fingers are slender and elegant, her tawny skin perfect and without blemish. Her nails are kept short but professionally manicured. Her nails are painted in a pale pink color that seems too whimsical for the confident, intelligent woman standing over me, and I'm getting the sense there's a lot more to Professor Garcia than meets the eye.

What I wouldn't give to have a chance to peel back some of those layers.

While she's been articulating the finer points of empirical and mathematical reasoning, I've been imagining how her hands would feel roaming all over my body and how supple and silky smooth her skin would feel under my fingertips. If I got her in bed, I wonder how much she'd arch that sexy body writhing underneath me. My pants grow tight, and I squirm self-consciously in my seat. I'm half-expecting campus police to show up and arrest me for my illicit fantasies. And honestly, with the thoughts I've been having about this woman lately, they *should* lock me up.

She sighs, shaking her head. "Are you always this distracted?"

No. Only with you. I don't say it. Obvs. Crushing on your prof is a big no-no, no matter how beautiful she is. Half the campus has a massive hard-on for her. Only last night, Duke admitted to rubbing one off after her class yesterday, so I'm certainly not alone in my lusting. Professor Garcia is the hottest professor on campus by a mile. She's certainly the youngest. Apparently, she was a bit of a child prodigy. Graduated high school at an impressively young age. Received her degree in strategy within three years and went on to complete an MBA straight afterward. She landed her position here two years ago, and she's been the talk of the campus ever since—she's inspired more wet dreams than I've had hot dinners.

The irony of this situation isn't lost on me. I'm only in need of tutoring because I zone out whenever I'm in her class, focusing on every part of her except for the words flowing out of her sexy mouth. Nothing of substance registers in my brain, and that's how I've fallen behind. Graduating top of my class is my primary goal—nothing less will be acceptable to Mom. She has big plans for me when I graduate. A frown forms naturally with my current line of thinking. For so long, all I aspired to was a management position in the family business, but lately, I've been questioning everything. Especially that.

Prof Garcia narrows her eyes as she stares at me expectantly. Frustration seeps out of her pores. Too lost in my head, I'd kinda forgotten she was still waiting for an answer. I'm no doubt testing her patience to the limit. "No, of course not. No one could accuse you of being boring. I, ah, didn't sleep well last night."

A vivid recollection of Tiffani's soft red curls and fake tits swims in front of my vision as details of last night resurrect with the worst timing known to mankind. I swore after our most recent hook-up it would be the last, but Tiffani doesn't take kindly to the word "no." She always waits until I'm buzzed and horny to approach me, knowing I'm too vulnerable to reject her advances.

It's pathetic to admit I'm ruled by my dick, but it's starting to ring true.

Tiffani represents everything I don't want for myself, but lust clouds my better judgment every damn time. And I'm not being fair to her either. She's still holding out hope that I'll concede to dating when I know that's never going to come to fruition.

"Get your head out of your ass, Mr. Kennedy," the professor hisses, surprising the hell out of me with her unapologetic tone. I damn near choke on a laugh. "Or we're done here before we've even begun."

It sounds like the starting line to a cheesy song, but I nod my head vigorously, not wanting to mess up this opportunity for a whole heap of reasons.

"Fine. I'll give you one more chance," she relents, hugging a stack of files to her magnificent tits. The platinum band on the fourth finger of her left hand glistens and sparkles under the overhead light, and it's a timely reminder that *she's off limits* in more ways than one. Rumor has it she got married at eighteen to some old dude, but I don't know if there's any shred of truth to it. She opens her mouth to say something when we're interrupted by a firm knock on the door.

Her brows nudge up. "You're expecting company in the middle of a planned study session?"

"No!" I rush to reassure her before she changes her mind and cancels the whole thing. "I'm not expecting anyone. They must have the wrong room." I push out of my chair, stretching to my full height. I tower over her petite frame, and that makes me feel all alpha-protector-like. "I'll get rid of them."

She waves her hand dismissively in the air. "It's fine. I was leaving anyway." She flips the lock on her briefcase and strides across the hardwood floor toward the door.

I catch up, whipping the door open first. There's no one there, so I poke my head out, scanning left and right. My brow creases in concern when I spot my cousin and Brad. "Faye?" I call out.

She spins on her heel, a sheepish look on her pretty face. "Surprise!" she says in her cute Irish accent.

"What are you doing here?"

"I need to speak to Keven about something, but if this is a bad time..." She smiles over my shoulder, and I need to shut this down. Right. Now.

"No. It's fine. Professor Garcia was just leaving." I step sideways to allow her to exit.

"Same time next Saturday, Mr. Kennedy," she says primly. Her thick, dark hair sways seductively over her shoulders, and it takes enormous willpower not to track the movement. Out of the corner of my eye, I spy Brad smirking.

"Thank you. I'll see you then," I mumble without looking at her, gesturing my guests into the room.

Faye wanders around the room, checking out the place while Brad stays beside me. He cocks his head to the side, still smirking. "Scored some private lessons?"

"She's one of my professors, asshat! And she's married." I slam the front door shut with more force than necessary.

"She's clearly *very* dedicated to turn up so early on a Saturday," he says, determined to milk this. He flops onto one of the couches, stretching out like he owns the place.

"Make yourself at home, Brad," I snap, "and drop the insinuation. I don't appreciate it." Because it's far too close to the bone. It's one thing to lust after someone you can't have from a distance and quite another to resist the craving up close and personal. I know I need her help if I'm to improve my grade, but I don't know how the hell I'm going to control myself in her presence.

This is from Chapter 30 of Losing Kyler and it shows some of the courtroom scene narrated from Kalvin's point of view.

♥♥♥♥♥♥

I keep my gaze dead ahead despite how every cell in my body strains toward her—like an invisible piece of string pulling tight between us. I can't remember the last time I've gone this long without seeing Lana. Without talking to her. Despite what she's doing to me, despite the fear and the pain, I can't stop myself from missing her like crazy. I should hate her, but I can't find it in myself to. My fingers dig into the edge of the glossy mahogany table as my heart pounds expectantly in my chest.

The judge enters the courtroom, and then my attorney is nudging me subtly into my seat. I still don't look over at her. I'm afraid to. Afraid of all the emotions it will drag to the surface. My life is on the line here today, and I've got to hold it together. One look at Lana and my carefully constructed façade will crumple.

The court dissolves into hushed murmurings when Lana is called to give evidence. I knew this was coming, and I thought I was prepared, but the second I hear her sweet voice, I rock back in my chair, accosted by a rush of conflicted emotions. I feel so many things for this girl. What a pity I hadn't realized exactly how much before I hurt her so completely she felt compelled to lie in retaliation.

I keep my eyes glued to the top of the desk as the prosecutor starts his line of questioning. They start off nice and easy, and it isn't hard to detect the underlying note of joy in her voice when she talks of our childhood. My mind easily resurrects the memories: Summers spent kiss-chasing in the grounds of our house, fooling about in the pool as we desperately tried to dunk one another, and eating ice cream and drinking Greta's pink lemonade while stretched out on sun loungers, pretending to sun bathe and feeling so grown up. Her tone turns slightly wistful when she mentions visiting Nantucket, and I can imagine her cheeks are burning up at the thought of her last trip there.

We were thirteen and it was the first time I kissed her. Properly kissed her. Not like our kiss-chasing escapades that were more giggling and lame half-assed sloppy kisses than any real attempt to make out. That whole vacation was different. Hormones had been buzzing in my veins, and I'd been thinking about nothing else but kissing her from the minute we arrived at our house. She was sorting her bag for the return trip when I walked into her room and boldly kissed her. No warning. I just stomped up to her, bent down, and pressed my lips to hers. I can still see the shock splayed across her face. Still taste how soft and warm her lips felt against mine. It had been over almost as fast as it had begun because Mom walked into the room and caught us. Failing to disguise the look of absolute horror on her face, she had told me in a clipped tone of voice to go and pack up my things.

That was the last time Lana was invited to Nantucket with us, and thinking back on it now, the start of when everything went wrong.

I force myself to tune back into the current conversation, shaking all other thoughts from my mind. No good will come from thinking about all that shit now.

"At this time, Ms. Taylor, what were your feelings toward the defendant, Mr. Kalvin Kennedy?" the prosecutor asks, and I do the unthinkable. I lift my head up, taking my first look at her.

She looks tired and gaunt, like the weeks and months in between have taken a toll on her too. Her hair is pulled back in a harsh, tight ponytail, and her face is makeup-free, but she's still the most beautiful girl I've ever seen. I know every inch of that face intimately from the smattering of tiny freckles across her nose to the slight scar transcending her right eyebrow, the result of her tripping over her book bag and falling headfirst into the sharp corner of the door.

Most every childhood memory I have links back to her. The entire fabric of my life is so intertwined with Lana's that I don't know how to exist without her.

A familiar pink stain is coloring her pale cheeks as she looks in my direction. Her warm hazel eyes don't falter as she replies. "I was in love with him. I'd always been in love with him, but when I was younger, I hadn't been able to put a name to it."

I can totally relate.

"And how did Mr. Kennedy feel about you?"

I can't look away now, even if I wanted to. Our eyes stay locked as she responds. "He told me he loved me too."

I do. I still do.

"So, you two were in a relationship then," the prosecutor paraphrases, pacing in front of the witness box.

Her mouth turns down, and my insides bunch into knots. "Not exactly."

"Can you please elaborate for the court."

"He, ah." She stops to take a drink of her water. "He wanted to keep our relationship secret."

To protect you! To keep you safe from all those who would say you weren't good enough for me. Which is fucking ironic, because it was completely the other way. I've never been worthy of her.

The prosecutor turns around, facing me head-on with a look of perplexed surprise. What a fucking jackass. As if anyone is buying this clearly orchestrated scene. He relinquishes his gaze, turning around to Lana again. "And why was that?"

She averts her eyes, and I feel bereft without the intensity of her gaze. "He said it was to protect me, because others wouldn't approve of us being together."

And I was telling the truth.

"And you believed him?" The prosecutor quirks a brow, and Lana nods.

"You need to answer the question, Ms. Taylor," the judge instructs.

"Yes," Lana says, staring at me again. "I believed him."

I want to jump up and tell her it was no word of a lie. That everything I said and did was to protect her. That all I'm guilty of is getting drunk and letting that slut Addison take advantage of me. And, yes, I know I should've resisted. Buzzed or not, I should've known better. For the rest of my life I will never forgive myself for that night. Never.

"And was this relationship an exclusive one?" the prosecutor asks next.

Her cheeks predictably flare up, and the urge to leap to her defense is a hard one to quash. After years of protecting her, it's like second nature to me.

"Not at first, but then he promised me he was finished with other girls. That was when he told me he loved me." She shifts uncomfortably in her chair, gazing at her lap and avoiding eye contact with anyone.

"Other girls?" The prosecutor pins me with a shocked look, and my middle finger twitches under the seat.

Lana sighs, moving uneasily in her chair. "Kal was… is a player. There have been plenty of other girls."

Humiliation crushes me at her words. Words I can't deny. It's amazing how it only takes one life-threatening moment to put everything into perspective. I've had plenty of time on my hands these last couple of months to assess how I was living my life. There isn't much to like about the person I've become. I'm an ass. Straight-up Douchey McDouche. Thought I could bang my way around town without any consequence. Happily hooked up with any girl willing to spread her legs for me thinking I was fucking cool. Fucking pathetic more like. The fact that I'd convinced myself I needed to get it all out of system before committing to the one girl—the only girl—I'll ever give my heart to doesn't in any way excuse my behavior. It just makes me more of an asshole.

"And how did that make you feel?" the prosecutor continues, and I wish Dr. Who would magically appear, jump out of the Tardis, and whisk me away from here before I hear her reply.

Lana eyeballs me. "Worthless. Invisible. Cheap."

Important. Significant. Precious. She could take a knife to my insides, and it wouldn't hurt as much. Even if I lived ten lifetimes, there is nothing I can do to make her realize how she is the complete opposite of all those things, because she'll never believe another word that comes out of my mouth.

"And was this before or after he promised you exclusivity?" The fuckwit attorney continues to stick the knife in deep.

"Before. When I tried to break things off with him, and I explained how it was making me feel, he told me he'd stop sleeping around. That he'd commit to me."

And I did, Lana. I did.

"And what happened then?"

"He was more dedicated, and he seemed to be trying to prove he had changed his ways. I was happy." Her eyes glisten, and it kills me. "He told me he loved me and I was the only girl for him. That he'd always imagined us together. That I was his future." A tear rolls down her face and all I can do is stare, horrified.

She *is* the only girl for me. I never lied about that. About any of that. I had our future all mapped out, and I never entertained thoughts that it wouldn't come to pass.

"What happened next?" The prosecutor is relentless, and I'd love to get up and smack him in the mouth.

Lana's eyes briefly shutter. Her lip trembles, and that primal urge to rush to her side to comfort her is riding me hard again. Kent would have a field day if he could read my mind. He hasn't stopped spewing crap about Lana from the minute this shit hit the fan, not that I expect him to understand. He is incapable of loving another living thing. Ky, on the other side of the spectrum, has been surprisingly understanding. Or maybe it's not altogether unsurprising. He's lost the girl he loves too, so he knows what this feels like. It doesn't matter that Lana has done this. Brought us to this point, because, the way I see it, she hasn't done this.

I have.

I drove her to do this.

It's all on me.

And even if I go down for this, for something I didn't do, I won't ever blame her.

I love her.

I only wish it hadn't taken me so long to fully realize it.

♥♥♥♥♥♥♥

END OF LOSING KYLER BONUS CONTENT

Loving Kalvin
(The Kennedy Boys Book 5)

A friends-to-lovers second-chance romance from USA Today bestseller Siobhan Davis. Standalone with HEA and no cliff hanger.

Lana

I knew it would end in disaster, but I didn't listen to reason. I didn't care. Because I loved him so much.

Kalvin Kennedy ruled my heart.

Until he destroyed it.

Shattered it so completely that I became someone else. Someone I loathed. Someone who repeatedly lied to her loved ones.

So, I ran.

From him. From myself. Desperate to hide my new reality.

But I could only run so far.

When he reappears in my life, I'm terrified. Unbelievably scared of facing the consequences of my actions.

Never mind that I still love him and want him so badly—there's too much at stake now.

How can I trust him with the biggest secret of all when he's likely to rip my world apart again?

Kalvin

Lana was always far too good for me. Everyone knew it but her.

I tried to stay away, but I was weak.

And I hurt her.

Crushed her until she barely resembled herself. Forced her to follow a path she would never have willingly chosen.

And then she was gone.

And my world has never felt as empty, as lonely.

She begged me to stay away. Not to find her. To forget she ever existed.

But that's like asking me to slice my heart in two and toss half aside.

I've never believed in fate, but when I rock up to the University of Florida, I'm ready to eat my words.

Because she's here. Like I hoped she would be. And I'm determined to prove I deserve a second chance.

TURN THE PAGE TO READ A SAMPLE FROM THIS BOOK *and SAVING BRAD*.

Loving Kalvin Sample

Prologue
November Trial

Lana

I used to think I was a decent person.

Kind, mostly selfless, with a good sense of morality, a good heart.

But I was clearly mistaken.

Because a good, kind, selfless person doesn't do the things I've done these last couple months.

A good person wouldn't continue to lie.

A good person wouldn't accuse the only boy who's ever mattered of such a horrible thing.

"Lana, we need to leave in thirty minutes to ensure we get parking outside the courthouse," Mom says, poking her head through the door. She checked us into adjoining rooms in the hotel because she's terrified to let me out of her sight these days.

I look up from the desk, chewing on the corner of my pen. "Okay. I'll be ready."

Her expressive hazel eyes—so similar to my own—flit to the handwritten page in front of me. Straightening up, she levels a stern look at me. "What are you doing?"

"I'm writing Faye a letter," I lie with the confidence of an expert deceiver. The lies just flow off my tongue like warm butter sliding off a knife these days.

I'm a total fraud, and I couldn't hate myself any more if I tried.

I swallow the painful lump in my throat as I offer her a brittle smile.

"Why? You don't owe that girl anything." Her lips pull into a tight line.

"Don't, Mom." I shake my head. "She was my friend, and I owe her an explanation."

"I beg to differ." Mom crosses her arms over her chest. "Today is all the explanation she needs. Once you testify, she'll understand exactly why you left without clarifying what happened. It was better that way. Leave it alone, darling."

Nausea swims up my throat, and I doubt I'll get through today without hurling. I could continue arguing with her, but then I won't get my letter finished. And it's too important to rush. "Mom, please. I don't want to fight. Not today. I'm writing my friend a letter, and then I'll put my suit on"—I gesture toward the black, shapeless monstrosity she laid out on the bed earlier—"and meet you in the lobby before we need to leave."

Clearly noting the resolve in my tone and my expression, she backs down. "I don't want to fight with you either, honey. I know how difficult today is going to be. I'll leave you to write your letter in peace." She closes the door quietly behind her.

I collapse in my chair, exhaling loudly.

Yes, today is going to be difficult.

But not for the reason she thinks.

Shaking aside those thoughts, I refocus on the task at hand. I examine the heap of crumpled pages in the trash—testament to more epic failure. For someone who aspires to be a writer, it's pathetic that I can't find the right words to tell the boy I love how sorry I am. I know him inside and out, so this should be uncomplicated. Shoot straight from the heart. *Cakewalk, right?*

So, why is this one of the hardest things I've ever had to do?

Glancing at the half-written page in front of me, I scan my latest effort with a frown. Frustrated, I scrunch the page into a ball and toss it clear across the room.

Ugh. Propping my elbows on the desk, I drop my head into my hands and shut my eyes.

His hauntingly beautiful face dances across the fields of my imagination, and a deep pang of yearning punches another hole in my heart.

Gosh, I miss him so much, and I'm not sure I have the strength to do this.

The problem is simple really.

I *could* write this letter, but I don't want to.

That's what's holding me back.

Even though I know it's for the best, there's a romantic, nostalgic part of me that still sees Kalvin Kennedy as my Prince Charming. My Mr. Right. My future.

The issue with that picture isn't Kal. Not really. Although, I'm sure he must hate me now, but this one is on me.

It's all my fault.

I wish things were different.

I wish I could rewrite our story, but I can't. The damage is done, and there's no going back.

The usual panic waylays me. I take deep breaths. In and out. Reminding myself I'm doing the right thing. And I can do this.

I'm strong enough.

I'll have to be.

I rub a tense spot between my brows, picking up the pen and a new piece of paper. I squint at the clock. Time is ticking. It's now or never.

Kal,

Writing this letter has been one of the most difficult things I've ever done. I never thought the time would come when words were the obstacle lying between us.

I'm sorry has never seemed more inadequate than it does in this moment. I could fill this page with row upon row of apologies, and it still wouldn't come close to making up for what I have done to you, so, I won't go there. Just know there is no word in the English language that can convey how truly regretful I am.

I don't think a day will pass where you aren't hijacking my mind because you live there—in my thoughts and in my dreams. Sometimes, in my nightmares.

You are all I think about, even when I'm trying so hard to forget you.

Even now. Even after all the hurt and the pain, I still love you so much. Probably too much for someone my age. I used to believe it was because we were made for each other. That we had a special kind of love most people never find. Now, I wonder if it's the opposite. If we were put together to show the destructive side of love.

*You have always been my light **and** my dark.*

*My sun **and** shadow.*

*My strength **and** weakness.*

*You bring out the best **and** the worst in me.*

Your continual rejection over the years hurt me more than you know— yet it was nothing compared to the pain I endured when Addison showed me that video.

It hurt, Kal. It hurt so much.

I've never experienced that kind of soul-crushing pain before. Not even when you first brushed me aside, and I thought I wanted to die.

It's not an excuse for how I've behaved, and I'm not presenting it as such—I'm merely stating the facts, so you can try to understand where this stemmed from.

I've gone over and over it in my mind, and most days I struggle to connect my actions with the person I know I am. It's like a stranger inhabited my body, and I allowed her full control. Unbearable pain blindsided me, separated me from my soul and my heart, and I trusted in someone who manipulated me. I should have known better. I did know better.

I've rewritten this letter a hundred times, and it's tempting to leave out the most important fact, but there's no point in writing a letter without *honesty. I knew it would hurt you, and I wanted you to <u>hurt as much as I was.</u>*

There. I've said it. Now you know how truly awful I am.

I don't feel that way anymore, and I'm ashamed I acted so rashly, that I caused so much pain, but I can't undo what I've done. I can only try and repair the damage and hope that, in time, you can somehow find it in your heart to forgive me. Because the thought of you living the rest of your life hating me is worse than the prospect of living mine without you by my side.

Mom claims I have an old soul. Maybe that's why I was always so sure about us. Why our age never made a difference. Why my love felt like it was born of decades not years. Perhaps that illusion of love shielded me from facing reality.

You and I aren't meant to be.

I will never regret the time we spent together. Precious childhood memories will remain untarnished in my mind, but that future we both dreamed about as kids was a fallacy created by fertile imaginations.

It's got to be. Because otherwise we would not have ended up here.

A sneaky tear slips out of my eye, rolling in slow motion down my face. It lands on the page, blurring the ink a little. I swipe under my eyes with my thumbs, glancing at the clock. I resume writing before I run out of time or my nerve fails.

I love you. I always have and I always will, but I'm letting you go. It's best for everyone involved.

Dream big, Kal, because you are destined for great things.

Don't look for me.

If you've ever cared for me, you will do that one thing. You will stay away. Leave the past in the past, and pretend like I never even existed.

But remember this much—you are the only boy who ever owned a piece of my heart, and that piece will always belong to you.

I will never forget you.

Be happy.
Lana.

The tears return as I fold the page, fit it into an envelope, and write his name on the front. More quiet tears fall as I shuck off my pajamas and pull on the austere jet-black skirt suit. I button the crisp, white shirt all the way up to my neck as I toe on my ballet flats. Tucking the letter safely into the inside pocket of my jacket, I vow to find some way of getting this to Faye before the end of the day. She's the only one I trust to deliver it to him.

I smooth my long, dark hair into a tight ponytail, taking one last look in the mirror before I leave.

I look like I'm attending my own funeral.

Which is pretty ironic, because that's exactly what it feels like as I vacate my hotel room for the final time.

Chapter One
October of the following year

Lana

My head is buzzing, and it feels good. Feels great.

I'm doing it.

Thrusting my bottle of beer at Olivia, I stride toward the bar on slightly shaky legs, determined to properly let loose. This is the third time we've attended the Kappa Sigma Friday night party, and every other time I've wanted to do this, I've chickened out.

Not tonight.

Tonight, I have my big girl pants on.

The few beers I downed earlier at the Gator Growl—UF's flagship event which marked the culmination of all the homecoming week activities—have helped loosen my inhibitions, too.

"Lana?" Olivia tugs on my elbow. "What're you doing?"

"I'm dancing," I confirm, kicking off my shoes. My roommate gawks at me, and I flash her a crooked grin.

Friday night is the only free time I have during the week, my one and only opportunity to cut loose, and I'm determined to make the most of it tonight.

I skip toward the bar area at the rear of the basement. This whole space was purpose-built a few years ago from a generous ex-frat alumni donation, if rumors are to be believed. The other side of the basement houses a few pool tables, a foosball table, a bunch of bean bags and low couches, and a top-notch stereo system. I stuck my head in that room one time and almost passed out from the pungent smoke infusing the air. This section is where most of the drinking and dancing takes place, and I'm way more comfortable out here.

I've never been a big drinker, but I allow myself a couple drinks on Fridays, as a reward of sorts for working my ass off all week.

A large counter runs the length of the wall at the back. Rows of shelves are built in behind it with designated space for kegs and cubbyholes stacked full of cups and other drinking paraphernalia. It's not a functional bar, but it's the next best thing.

These parties are legendary, and everyone wants an in. Riley—the junior Liv recently started dating—lives here, so we're an automatic shoo-in now.

The dancing on the bar tradition was started a couple years back by a few seniors—girls from a nearby sorority—who gatecrashed one night. They started a trend, and now it's almost as legendary as the parties themselves.

The old me wouldn't have dreamed of doing anything so wild.

The new me can't wait to get my ass up on that counter. Tonight, I'm joining the honorary roll call, consequences be damned.

I haul myself up on the bar, rather inelegantly, staggering a little until I find my balance. A loud cheer erupts from the packed crowd when I remove my shirt and toss it in Olivia's direction. My white tank top is tight with thin straps and a sheer lace overlay which touches the edge of my short jean skirt. My usual pale skin is tan from a summer spent by the pool on the grounds of my grandparents' lavish property.

My hips move of their own accord, and I glance sideways, sharing a blinding smile with the petite redhead dancing alongside me. We grin at each other as the slick beats pump out. Flinging my hair over my shoulders, I do a little shimmy up and down, earning a few catcalls in the process.

I notice a couple of guys watching my every move, and my skin heats up. My moves become a little more provocative, a little sexier. Out of the corner of my eye, I catch Liv smiling in my direction. She gives me a quick thumbs-up, and I laugh, continuing to pump and grind to the sultry rhythm.

Surprisingly, I'm enjoying this.

The old Lana would never have been so uninhibited.

But that girl no longer exists.

Along with her scandalous past.

I'm not Lana Taylor anymore. Courtesy of my wealthy grandparents, and a recent circuit court petition, I'm now Lana Williams. A new name deserves a new outlook on life, and I'm determined to forge a new path. To forget the boy who forever captured my heart on a beach in Nantucket.

A surge of guilt washes over me. It's the same any time I think of Kal. Which is mostly every day, so, obviously, I haven't been entirely successful with banishing my past, but it's a work in progress. I'm determined to move beyond it.

Otherwise, what was the point of it all?

The redhead nudges my hip, and I realize I've stopped dancing. Forcing all thoughts of Kalvin Kennedy from my mind, I immerse myself in the song, dancing my punctured little heart out.

Sweat trickles down my spine, and my mouth is dry as sandpaper. I'm thinking of calling it quits when I'm distracted by the sound of roaring and clapping coming from the far right-hand side of the room. A group of football players are huddled in a circle, raising their beers in a united salute. As the crowd disperses, I notice the boy and girl descending the stairs into the basement, and my heart stutters in my chest.

She is model beautiful with thick, glossy blonde locks, killer curves, and long limbs. More than a few heads turn in her direction, but I've stopped noticing her because the boy beside her has just sent my world into a tailspin.

"No!" I gasp, and my knees turn to Jell-O. With my stomach lurching, and my legs almost buckling, I sway precariously on the counter as everything crashes down around me.

I'm going to be sick.

His head is angled toward the bar, and my mind switches off. I dive off the counter, uncaring how or where I land. I just know that I need to get out of his line of sight before he spots me.

My heart is jackhammering against my ribcage as I flail about in the air. A pair of strong, muscular arms catch me before I face-plant the ground. "Whoa there, pretty lady!" a deep, rich voice says. "You fall or something?" my savior asks, repositioning me so I'm cradled against his very broad, very warm chest.

I peer into lush chocolate-colored eyes, blinking profusely. "Sorry!" I attempt to wriggle out of his hold, but he tightens his grip on my waist.

"You sure you're okay?"

"She's fine," Liv says, materializing alongside us. "You can release her now, Chase."

Chase frowns as he carefully places my bare feet on the ground. Olivia hands me my shoes, eyeing the guy suspiciously. With her abnormally tall frame, flawless dark skin, striking eyes, and thick jet-black hair, Olivia can command a room like no other girl I know. She's like this fierce Amazonian warrior, reminding me of those stunning female vampires from *Twilight*.

I'm dwarfed when I stand beside her, scrawny and small, the contrast between us never more transparent. Perhaps that's why she's taken such a protective stance. Why she looks out for me even when I don't ask her to.

Chase regards her warily, scrubbing a hand over his stubbly jaw. "Do I know you?"

"Nope, but your rep precedes you."

He grins, showcasing a set of cut dimples. "Don't believe everything you hear."

"Uh-huh." My roomie pins him with a wary look.

Chase chuckles, raising his palms in the air. "Hey, I was just doing my good deed for the night. No ulterior motives." He turns to me, his eyes roaming up and down my body as I toe on my shoes. "None, whatsoever." He winks, and heat floods my cheeks. I'm unaccustomed to such shameless flirting, and it throws me for a loop. "Not like I was watching your pretty friend rock that counter like she belongs on stage or anything." His grin widens, and my cheeks burn brighter.

Straightening up, I clear my throat. "Thank you. For catching me."

He takes my hand in his meatier one, drawing it to his mouth. "The pleasure was all mine. Anytime …" He quirks a brow.

"I'm Lana."

He plants a soft kiss on the back of my hand. "Nice to meet you, Lana." Leaning in, he presses his ear to my mouth. "I definitely hope we meet again." A slew of shivers ripple over my skin as his warm breath tickles my neck.

He sends me one final cheeky wink before disappearing into the heaving crowd.

"That one is trouble," Liv warns.

Mention of trouble brings me back into the moment. Grabbing my shirt and purse, I tug on her arm. "Come on. We need to leave. Now."

"Where's the fire?"

I risk a quick peek over her shoulder, emitting a high-pitched shriek. He's heading our way, and if we don't get our butts out of here right this second, everything I've worked for will be shot to hell. Olivia turns to look at the object of my distraction. "No! Don't look at him. He'll see you!" I yank on her arm again.

"What the hell, Lana?" She slants a puzzled look my way.

"I'll explain everything when we get back to the dorm, but we have to go. Please, Liv. I'm begging you. We have to go *now*." Hysteria is bubbling to the surface as the words leave my mouth, and butterflies are running amok in my chest.

"'Kay. Quick."

We start pushing our way through the crowd. My tank top is glued to my back, and tiny beads of sweat have formed on my brow.

He can't see me, he just can't.

Olivia guides me to a side exit at the back of the bar. We shove through the door, barreling out into a narrow alleyway at the back of the building. I run toward the steep stone steps, ignoring the sounds of heavy make-out sessions happening all around us.

"Lana!" a familiar voice calls out, and I whimper. Dammit all to hell.

"Keep running," Olivia commands, racing hot on my heels. Fueled by adrenaline, I bound up the stairs, pushing my limbs harder than ever before, such is my desire to outrun him.

"Lana! Wait!" The voice is distant, but it won't take him long to catch up.

We race around the corner of the building. "Follow me." Olivia veers off to the right. I give chase as she maneuvers a curved path through the shrubbery in between various frats, weaving in and out of houses like it's her own personal obstacle course. Under the dark blanket of nightfall, I stumble several times as I struggle to keep up. My breath hisses out in panicked spurts, but I resist the urge to look over my shoulder as I race after Liv.

We emerge on one of the main roads, a few yards from a bus stop. "Hold the bus!" Liv screeches as the last passenger ascends the vehicle parked at the curb. We tear down the sidewalk and hop onto the bus in the nick of time. Panting, I scan my card and scurry behind Olivia, dropping into a seat alongside her.

"That was cutting it close," I pant, desperately trying to get my breathing and my heart rate under control.

"I'll say." She shoots me a curious look, before glancing out the rear window of the bus. It takes considerable willpower to keep my focus straight ahead.

A couple of minutes pass in silence, as we both bring our breathing back in line.

I sigh. My head is a mess, and my slightly inebriated state isn't helping either. Anxiety is holding me hostage, and I can't think straight.

What the hell is he doing here?

Olivia bumps my shoulder. "You said there was a guy."

"Yes."

I told her there was a guy, but I deliberately avoided divulging the details. I had good reasons not to. Plenty of them. Liv and I gelled the instant we met, and I didn't want her thinking any less of me. Now, there's no avoiding it. I owe her an explanation, and I'm not going to lie.

I've already told a lifetime of lies.

Liv isn't prone to rash judgments, and I know she'll give me the floor to explain. I hope it's enough. Wetting my dry lips, I study her calm expression.

"When were you going to tell me it was Kalvin Kennedy?" she asks.

Chapter Two

Kalvin

"Goddammit!!" I yell in frustration, coming to a halt as I watch the bus pull away from the curb. Dropping onto a nearby bench, I rest my head in my hands. Adrenaline is coursing through my body, and my heart is thundering in my chest.

She. Is. Here!

When I first caught a glimpse of the crazy girl nose-diving off the bar, my heart stuttered at the mere possibility that it might be her. Well, that and the fear that she'd go splat on the floor. Then I lost her in the crowd, especially when Shelby stopped to talk to some jerk from her anthropology class. It was only when Lana's considerably taller friend started rushing her out the side exit that I got another look. I only saw her from behind, but I knew. I knew it was her, even if her hair is longer than I've ever seen it and the clothes she was wearing were nothing like my Lana used to wear.

I only needed that teeny, tiny glimpse to know it was her.

You never forget the girl who claimed your heart. Even if she did it without me realizing.

It took our lengthy separation for me to see her in the right light.

To know I loved her more than I loved anyone or anything in the entire universe.

I didn't know love until it tore up my heart. Until I was all cut up inside. Until the loss consumed me, and I could barely breathe without her. It's only then I realized I'd do anything to get her back.

Kill. Maim. Injure. Beg. Borrow. Steal.

There isn't anything I'm unprepared to do to win Lana back.

Fuck me. I'm turning into my pansy-ass brother. Lying flat on my back on the bench, with my knees bent, I laugh my ass off as relief cascades over me like a waterfall.

She enrolled, after all. Thank fuck.

My laughter dies off, replaced by a heady surge of longing.

I can hardly believe it.

I've been on campus for two months now, and I spent the first few weeks scouring the place for any sign of Lana. I had no idea how vast the University of Florida was or how trying to find one girl on a two-thousand-acre campus was virtually impossible. Although, it doesn't seem as big now that I know my way around a bit better. After weeks of roaming the campus like an aimless idiot, I finally succumbed and called my brother. Keven has mad IT skills, and it didn't take him long to hack into the college servers and search the considerable student database only to draw a blank.

My heart had sunk when he confirmed there was no Lana Taylor registered.

I'd been so sure she'd come here. I knew she had enough credits built up to skip senior year, like me, and she'd had her heart set on UF. I remembered the times we'd talked about it, and it'd played no insignificant part in my decision to come here instead of attending Harvard with my brothers and my cousin.

Although this is one of the top universities in the country, and their architecture program is dope, I came here for *her*.

A goofy smile appears on my lips.

For the first time in over a year, I feel alive. The urge to pull a Leo and shout "I'm the king of the world" is riding me hard. Damn my wacky Irish cousin Faye and her stupid *Titanic* fixation. That girl has messed with my brain in a big way.

If anyone found me now—lying on a bench, in the pitch dark, in the middle of the night, laughing to myself—they'd have me carted off to the nearest psychiatric ward before I could draw a breath.

My knee bounces up and down, and I'm chock-full of nervous excitement. I desperately need to track Lana down. If I knew where to begin,

I'd be on it in a flash. It feels like an eternity since I last spoke to her, and I crave her company as intensely as a druggie craves his next fix.

To have come so close is killing me.

However, I refuse to feel anything but pure excitement.

Lana is here. That is all that matters.

This changes *everything*.

I may have lost her just now, but I'm not giving up until I find her. Until I speak to her and convince her I'm finally in the right place. Ready to give her a commitment and mean it this time.

I haul myself upright and make my way back to the frat house.

"Hey, is everything okay?" Shelby asks, the second I reappear in the room.

The music is blaring and the crowd is getting rowdy. Most of us have been partying since the event earlier, and things are turning messy. I've been making a concerted effort to keep my nose clean. Party-boy Kal is a thing of the past, and I'd rather not hit a speed bump.

Shelby palms my face in concern. That's another thing I'll need to deal with but not now. Now, I need to drag Brett's ass out of here and force him to help me.

"Who was that girl?" she asks, peering up at me through her gorgeous big blue eyes. Shelby is every dude's wet dream, and I know I'd only have to say the words and she'd be mine, but that was never my intention. Even less so now. In the past, I wouldn't give two shits about screwing a girl one minute and ignoring her the next, but I'm not the same person I was. All the stuff that went down changed me. I'd like to think for the better.

"Someone important." That's as much as I'm saying on the subject.

Little lines crease her forehead. "Oh." She's not pleased.

"Look, I need to get out of here, but wanna meet for lunch tomorrow?" She deserves to be let down gently.

She perks up, and I feel like a dick. "Awesome. It's a date."

Double shit. "I'll text you in the morning."

She leans in to kiss me, and I twist my head at the last second so her lips meet my cheek instead of my mouth. Hurt flickers in her eyes, and I feel like a dick again. Over her shoulder, I spy Brett entertaining the adoring masses, and I catch his attention, gesturing toward the door.

My roomie nods, draining his beer and making a dash for it. "Please tell me we're not calling it a night, bro." He slaps me on the back. "I'm only getting started."

"We're not, but I need to talk to you. You want to shoot some pool?"

He steers me out of the room. "Lead the way, dude."

We grab an Uber to the local town and hop out in front of the combination sports bar and tavern. One of Brett's brothers attended UF a few years back, and he told us about this place.

They happily accept our fake IDs as the real deal, so we grab a couple of beers and slip into a booth while we wait for a pool table. Most Friday nights, this place is hopping, but it's quieter than usual tonight. The majority of the college crowd is still on campus, hitting up parties and enjoying the last festivities of homecoming week.

"What gives?" Brett asks, sipping from his beer.

"I found her. I just found Lana."

His eyes pop wide. "No shit."

"She was at the party, but she ran off before I could talk to her." I raise the bottle to my lips, enjoying the cold, bitter taste as the beer slides down my throat.

"What's the plan?"

"I'm going to get my brother on the case again. If she goes to school here, she must be registered under a different name." I lean my arm along the top of the booth. "Now that I know she's here, she can't hide from me."

"What if she was only visiting? She could have a friend here."

It's a legit argument, but it carries no weight. "She doesn't have any friends here. She grew up, with me, in Wellesley. Besides, it was always her dream to come here. She's enrolled at UF. I'm certain of it."

He props his arms on the table. "I still can't believe you traded Harvard—*Ivy League, dude*—for UF, on a hunch that some chick might attend."

"It was more than a hunch, and she's more than some chick." Brett isn't a fan of my girl, and he's starting to get on my last testicle. He's judging her—like the rest of the country—before he's even had the chance to know her. I take another quick glug of my beer. "The summer before we started high school, we discussed it. She told me she had her heart set on the University of Florida because she wanted to attend college in a sunnier climate and she wanted to connect with her grandparents. Her Mom never let her visit them."

"What's up with that?"

I shrug. "No idea, but it was important to her to be close to them. She had no other family."

He scratches the top of his head. "Dude, it's still weird. Who leaves their family behind to go on a wild goose chase? Just 'cause you discussed it a few years back was no guarantee she'd actually be here." His lips curve up. "Knew you had more than a little reckless in you."

I grin wickedly. "Dude, whatever, you're totally missing the point." I cock my head to the side. "I was right, because she *is* here, and that's all I give a crap about now. I *knew* she'd be here. Maybe my cuz is right." He arches a brow, waiting for elaboration. "Faye sa—"

"That's the hottie Irish chick you told me about? The one who's fucking your brother?"

I roll my eyes. "Yes, and yes, but you know it's not like that. Ky's my half-brother, and they're not actually blood related."

"It sounds much hotter the way I tell it." He smirks.

"Whatever gets you going, bro."

"You have any pictures of her?"

"Faye?"

"No, dipshit!" He taps his bottle against mine. "Your girl."

"Yeah." I remove my cell from my back pocket and hand it to him. My screensaver is a pic of Lana and me. It's the last happy image of us before everything turned to shit.

Brett whistles low on his breath. "She's pretty."

I grab my cell back, scoffing. "She's fucking gorgeous, but I don't expect you to understand everything she means to me."

He taps his fingers off the tabletop. "Enlighten me."

I pick at the label on my bottle. "I told you I spent years acting like a jerk. Pushing her away and pretending I didn't have feelings for her. Then I lost her, and my world lost all its color. When I get her back, I'm going to treat her like a fucking goddess."

"Pussy-whipped all ready," he murmurs, "and you don't even have the girl."

"Semantics, dude. That's all it is."

"Or a nasty case of overconfidence." His grin is teasing.

"I fucked up before, but I'm not going to do that again. I just need to make her understand that. She told me not to find her, so she's bound to be a bit pissed, but I'll use some of the ole Kennedy charm to win her around to my way of thinking." I'm spouting the biggest load of bullshit, but maybe if I say it out loud, I might start believing it. Truth is, I'm scared shitless that Lana will refuse to have anything to do with me. Can't say I blame her. Not after the years I spent acting like a complete moron.

And let's not forget how spectacularly I messed up with that bitch, Addison.

"You're a nice guy, Kal," Brett says, in a more serious tone of voice. "I'm not sure I'd be so understanding."

There'd been no need to tell Brett my story. When I rocked up to the dorms and met my new roomie, he recognized me instantly. That's what happens when your mom spearheaded one of the most prestigious, most recognizable fashion brands in the country. There was no such thing as privacy. My six brothers and I had grown up under the glare of the world's media. Last year was definitely one for the record books, though. Between my trial, my brother's arrest, my dad's affair, my cousin almost being killed, news that my three eldest brothers had a different father, and my mom's admission that she had lied to build her business empire on a falsehood, we were rarely off the airwaves. The media lapped the scandal up, and we were virtual pariahs at school.

Brett knew everything, which, to be honest, was freaking awesome, because it meant I didn't have to explain the shit show that is my life. More than that, he was understanding.

Except when it comes to Lana. That's where he draws a line.

When she came clean at the trial, she put herself in the spotlight, and it didn't present her in the most flattering light. Come to think of it, no wonder she registered under a different name. She probably didn't want anyone to know who she was. I'm sure she's picked up her fair share of enemies. That thought kicks my protective instincts into overdrive, accelerating the need to find and shelter her.

"She isn't how she was portrayed," I explain. "If anyone's to blame for what happened, it's me. Me and my brother's ex. Lana is a total sweetheart, and it was completely out of character for her to lie."

"I can tell you mean that. Like I said, you're one of the good guys."

"She means everything to me, man, and I let her down when she needed me most. It wasn't that difficult for me to forgive her. Fact, friend," I tag on the end, chuckling as I repeat Brett's catchphrase.

"She's a damn fool if she turns you away."

"It's not as simple as that."

I'll say.

Convincing Lana I forgive her for what she did is the least of it.

I have years of stupid mistakes to make up for.

And I can't wait to get started.

♥♥♥♥♥♥♥

Saving Brad
(The Kennedy Boys Book 6)

An enemies-to-lovers romance from *USA Today* bestselling author Siobhan Davis. Standalone with an HEA and no cliff-hanger.

Brad

I'm in love with my best friend's girl.

She knows it. He knows it. *Everyone* knows it.

Faye will never be mine, but try telling that to my stupid heart.

An endless rotation of girls streams in and out of my bedroom in a desperate attempt to forget her, but nothing eases the horrid ache in my chest. Rejection isn't anything new for me, but it hasn't gotten any easier.

Until *she* reappears in my life. Like an out-of-control tornado. Storming in, all fierce and angry, ready to steamroll everything in her path. Rachel is trouble with a capital T bundled in a gorgeous, sexy, Irish package.

She pushes all the wrong buttons, and I can't decide if I want to yell at her or kiss her.

I should steer clear.

But I've never been very good at taking my own advice. Especially when it comes to girls I can't have and shouldn't want.

Rachel

I need to escape.

To put as much distance between me and that monster so I can start living my life.

Yet, even the vast Atlantic Ocean isn't enough to sever the connection. To allow me to forget how he's ruined me. His hold is more than just physical. He has a vise-grip on my head and my heart, and I can't breathe, can't think, and can't function.

So, I do everything to blot it out.

Until *he* reappears in my life.

Brad McConaughey. So hot. So infuriating. So in love with my best friend.

Every word out of Brad's mouth makes me want to throat punch him or kick him in the nuts.

But he makes me *feel*, and I hate him for it. A part of me might actually love him for it.

I should keep my distance, but like destructive magnets, we are drawn together.

This isn't going to end well.

I know it. He knows it.

But we're powerless to resist.

**TURN THE PAGE TO READ YOUR EXCLUSIVE
SAMPLE FROM THIS BOOK.**

Saving Brad Sample

Prologue

August–Nantucket

Brad

"You remember Rach, right, Brad?" Faye gestures toward her friend who is currently engrossed in conversation on the other side of the patio with a newly engaged Lana and Kalvin. They've just returned from visiting the house Kal bought his fiancée as a surprise engagement present.

Hell, yeah. Of course, I remember her. "Sure." *Play it cool, dude.* "Hard to forget mouthy little Red." Except she's dyed her hair since the first time we met, and her bright red locks have been replaced by rich chocolaty-brown strands that beg to be touched.

Faye scowls. "I hope you're not going to be rude to her again."

Uh-oh. Recalling our chat from an hour ago, I realize it's a bit late for that. But that's not what Faye is referencing.

The first time I met Rachel was when she sprung a surprise visit on Faye, at Wellesley, with their other friend Jill, more than a year and a half ago.

I was only rude to her about ninety-five percent of the time.

The other five percent ... well, let's just say I definitely wasn't rude then and leave it at that.

I smother my smirk before Faye notices. "Don't worry. I'll play nice." I send her a toothy grin, and she narrows her eyes suspiciously. Considering Faye never said a word to me after her friends returned to Ireland, I think it's safe to assume Rachel didn't tell her what went down between us. I thought girls told each other everything, and I'd been expecting a shakedown that never happened.

Thoughts of that night wander through my mind, and not for the first time.

It was one of the hottest experiences of my life.

We'd been out in Boston earlier that day. After dinner in the city, we came back to the house and watched a couple of movies. Rachel and I had been knocking back beers at an alarming rate, as if it was an implied competition. Ky had been pawing at Faye relentlessly all day, and I'd just about reached my limit. Excusing myself, I'd lied and said I was tired, but I didn't head to bed. I stepped outside, oblivious to the cold winter night air because I was so consumed with thoughts of Faye and the caustic pain ripping my insides apart.

My heart throbs painfully in my chest, performing that horrible twisty thing it does every time I think of her—the girl I want and can never have.

Speaking of.

"Earth to Brad." Faye clicks her fingers in my face. "Where'd you go? I've been talking for, like, the last three minutes, and you haven't heard a word I said, have you?"

"Sorry. Drifted off."

She takes a step closer, and I instinctively take a step back. Defensive mode is the only way I can tolerate being around her these days. The urge to sweep her into my arms and kiss the living daylights out of her hasn't faded. Out of the corner of my eye, I spy Ky watching me with hawk eyes.

He knows.

He knows it hasn't gotten any better.

That I'm still lusting after his woman.

Wrong. Still in *love* with his woman.

The tiny cracks in our relationship are spreading, and I'm waiting for him to detonate. Can't say I'd blame my best bud. He's been unbelievably mature about the whole situation, but I know I'm stretching his patience to the limit. It's been almost two years, and I should be over her. God knows I've screwed enough girls in the intervening period, but trying to fuck her out of my head isn't working.

Nothing is working.

I'm still in love with my best friend's girl. His one true love. The girl who will always be by his side.

I'm pathetic and weak, and I hate myself for it. Every day my self-loathing intensifies until I think I might burn from the inside out.

Faye sighs, dragging me back into the moment. "Are things ever going to be okay with the three of us?" Her bright smile has evaporated.

I could lie but what's the point?

She knows how I feel.

He knows how I feel.

It's the unspoken elephant in the room. This constant wedge between us. I don't know how much more of the stress I can take.

"I'm trying," I answer honestly.

She shakes her head sadly. "No, you're not. Not really." I arch a brow. "I know you're screwing all around you, but you always pick the wrong girls, and I'll bet you're doing that on purpose."

"Don't try to psychoanalyze me," I growl, irritated all of a sudden. "You don't know what I'm feeling."

Bravely, she touches my arm. "You're right. I don't, because you keep shutting me out. Shutting Ky out."

"Because I have to!" I run my hands through my hair. "I can't talk to you about it, and you know why."

"You need to widen the field. Look for a nice girl, not one of those groupies who hang off your every word. That's not you. I know it isn't."

"Faye, I'm nineteen, on the football team at Harvard, and as horny as the next guy. No guy goes to college to find their soul mate. They go to party and fuck as many girls as they can before they settle down. There is nothing wrong with what I'm doing, and you and Kyler don't get to lecture me on my lifestyle, so butt out."

Shucking her hand off, I walk away, not giving a shit that it's rude to bail without warning. I need to blow off some steam—to calm the insanity brewing to epic proportions inside my head. I stomp down to the beach, veering left away from the party in full swing on the other side of the sandy strip.

I drop down onto the sand and rest my head on my knees. What an epic fuck-up. Shit. I let out a frustrated roar. Way to act like a total immature ass.

I need a distraction, so when my mind returns to that night with Rachel, I welcome it.

I was out on the patio, feeling sorry for myself when she joined me. "What do you want?" I snapped.

She faced the picturesque gardens as she spoke. "She's completely and utterly in love with Ky."

I sighed. "I know."

She turned around to me. "So, do something about it, because you're wasting your time if you think she's going to ever leave him."

"Don't pretend you know what I'm thinking or what I should do."

"You're an idiot." She barked out a laugh. "A guy like you has tons of options. Find someone else. Get laid. Find a life that isn't so centered around the Kennedys and this house. Take control of your own life. You dictate where you go and who you spend it with."

"You make it sound so easy." And, suddenly, I'd wondered if we were even speaking about me anymore.

She paused considerably before replying, and I swore tears appeared briefly in her eyes. "I know it's not easy. Nothing that important ever is."

"How do you do it?" I risked asking, looking at her with a fresh perspective.

Her pretty brown eyes glistened with pain. "I'm still trying to figure it out, but I think I'm getting there."

"How?" I whispered, moving closer to her. I stared deep into her eyes, like they might hold the key to eradicating my misery.

She peered up at me, contemplating how much to tell me. Right then, Rachel was an open book, and the pain I witnessed was all too real. That girl was hurting. "I drink and I fuck, usually in that order. It's the only time I can blank it all out."

My eyes popped wide in surprise. Not at what she told me. I'd seen enough the night before to verify that statement. I was startled she was being so honest. We were virtual strangers, and she owed me nothing. "Does it help?"

Her hand landed on my arm, and tingles danced over my skin even through my shirt. "Yes and no." *She moved closer and her chest brushed against mine.* "It dulls the pain in the moment." *Her hands slid up my chest, and my arms wrapped around her waist. My heart started beating faster.* "And in that moment, it feels fucking great. Not to think about any of the crap. Just to feel"—*she looked off into space*—"normal. Even if it is fleeting, delusional."

"You want to feel like that now?" *I whispered, fixating on her mouth so there could be no misunderstanding.*

"You don't even like me."

"You don't like me."

"True." *She smiled as her small hands crept around the back of my neck.* "You're a dick."

"Do you like most of the guys you fuck?" *I pulled her closer against my body, ensuring she felt the straining bulge in my pants.*

She thought about that for a bit. "No. Almost never."

I grinned. "Well then, I don't think we have any problem. Do you?" *A slight frown appeared on her forehead, and I instantly knew what caused it.* "Don't go there. You've already said it. She loves him. She wouldn't care about this."

"She cares about you."

"Please. Don't." *My tone was effusive with pleading. Now that the seeds had been sown, and my body was on board with the plan, if she backed out, I would be in a whole new world of pain.*

Removing her hands from my neck, she slid one down the narrow gap between us, palming my erection. "You need this? You need me?"

"Yes," *I growled, pushing into her hand.*

A steely resolve etched across her face. "Fuck me, Brad."

And I did.

And it was the hottest sex of my life.

Pushing her up against the wall, ensuring we were out of sight of the windows, I tore her panties away as she popped the button on my jeans. Our mouths meshed in a frantic marriage of pain and lust and anger and despair. She tasted of beer and mint, and her lips were as soft as silk as they moved effortlessly against mine. My fingers plunged into her wet warmth, and she moaned low under her breath, already as worked up as me. Shoving my jeans and boxers down, and quickly rolling a condom on, I thrust into her hard, over and over, while she dug her nails into my back. I captured her moans with my mouth and held her legs firmly around my waist as I fucked her. My hand was rough as it kneaded her breast through her dress, and I could feel her body on the brink of losing control. "God, Brad. Don't stop. Fuck me harder. Do it. Harder. Faster," she gritted out, and I damn near exploded on the spot. When she came, her entire body shuddered around me as she whispered my name in my ear. My release followed and I continued pumping until I was completely spent.

I'm hard now just thinking about it.

After we screwed, we just walked away without acknowledging what we'd done. She left the next day without even saying goodbye. I'd like to say I haven't thought of her in the interim, but there's no point lying to myself.

I have thought of her often.

Wondered what kind of pain tortures her.

Wondered how many random guys she's fucked since I last saw her and whether it's brought her any measure of peace.

I bark out a dry laugh as realization dawns. Unwittingly, I've been following her advice. Getting drunk and getting laid, but she's right. It's a momentary escape from the pain. Once it's over, the usual heartache returns. Only this time, the heartache is joined by a new layer of guilt and self-revulsion.

Does she feel that too?

Does Rachel hate herself as much as I hate me?

She's moving here now. She's transferred from her college in Ireland to the Massachusetts College of Art and Design. Alex Kennedy, Ky's mom, helped set everything up.

As Faye's best friend, and new roomie, Rachel is going to be a more permanent feature in my life. Not that I need any more complications, but I guess I'm about to discover the answers to my questions.

Chapter One
Three Weeks Later

Brad

Faye's stunning blue eyes swim to the forefront of my mind and I groan. *Not now. Go away.* It's bad enough I'm in love with my best friend's girl, but the fact she plays a starring role in my daily fantasies makes me feel like some sick pervert. Ky would cut my balls off if he knew the extent of my obsession. Honestly, it's getting to the stage where I'm starting to genuinely worry about myself. Nails dig into my ass, and I thrust harder, grunting as a wave of pleasure courses through me.

"Who the hell is Faye?" the blonde underneath me asks with a growl, clearly pissed.

"No one ..." *Fuck, what's her name? Cassie? Carla? Kayla, that's it, I'm pretty sure.* "Kayla. Sorry, baby. This is so good." I thrust in harder to drill it home. *See my point?* I'm totally losing it if I'm calling out Faye's name as I'm nailing some other chick. My own thoughts make me a little sick. *How has it come to this? How have I sunk so low?*

Her eyes roll in her head, and her back arches off the bed. "That *is* good, *baby*. And my name's Callie, asshole."

I pull her up onto my lap, bracing one arm against the headrest as I thrust my hips up to meet hers. I kiss her passionately, greedily, focusing one hundred percent on the hot blonde who is currently giving me the ride of my life. We went at it half the night, and I must've fallen asleep before I could kick her out. Not that I'm complaining. A morning quickie is a rare treat. My head dips, and I suck her nipple into my mouth. She screams my name out at the exact same moment the door to my bedroom swings opens.

"Ho. Lee. Crap!" a familiar voice shrieks, and I rip the blonde off me faster than a bloodsucking leech. "Shit, sorry, Brad. I didn't know you had company." Faye shields her face with her hand, quickly looking away. Her cheeks have turned bright red. You'd swear she was some virginal innocent by her obvious embarrassed expression. Except I share this apartment with her boyfriend, and I've heard them plenty of times in the throes of sex. Judging from the sounds emitting from his bedroom, and the way Ky's headboard bangs wildly against the wall, I'd say Faye is used to being well and truly fucked.

And now my mind has totally gone there. Great, just what I need. My dick starts hardening again, and I reach down, covering the evidence with my hands. The blonde grabs the sheet up under her chin, and her eyes beseech me to handle the situation.

"Faye, babe," Ky says, approaching from behind her. The blonde's eyes narrow suspiciously. Ky peers into the room, roaring with laughter as his hands snake around Faye's waist. He leans his chin on her shoulder. "You turned voyeur or something?"

She slaps his arm. "I didn't know he had someone in here."

"Eh, hello." I gesture toward Callie. "Do you mind getting the hell out of my room."

"Of course, bro." Ky starts backing Faye out into the narrow corridor. "But make it snappy. Rachel's flight lands at eleven, and we want to get there early in case it arrives ahead of schedule."

Dammit. I had totally forgotten today was the day. *Could this day get any worse? And why the hell did I agree to go with them?* I snort. I know why. Because Faye turned the charm on, and I relented straightaway. I'm wrapped around her finger every bit as much as Ky is.

They close the door, and I return my attention to Callie, my cock straining with renewed arousal. "Where are you going?" I reach for her as she swings her legs out the side of the bed.

"Home."

I pat the mattress. "Come back to bed. We have enough time to finish."

She plants her hands on her hips, standing before me stark naked, and damn, if it isn't hot as hell. She has a rocking body, and she isn't afraid to show it off. "I'm no longer in the mood."

I stand up, moving toward her with intent. "I can fix that in two seconds."

She thrusts out a palm, slamming into my chest and holding me at arm's length. She looks down at my hard erection. "I'll bet you could, but I'm not some dumb bimbo." She points at my dick. "That's not for me. That's for *her*." She spits the word out like it's poison.

"Ah come on, don't be like that." I make an attempt to pull her into me, but she's having none of it.

"I didn't want to believe everything that's said about you because I've seen how you are in class, and I couldn't reconcile that person with the rumors. But it turns out the rumors are true. You're a total douche, Brad, and nothing would entice me between the sheets with you again. Now, let me go."

I lift my hands in a conciliatory gesture. "Fine. Your loss." Guess I'll have to rub one out in the shower now.

She angrily pulls her clothes on as I grab a pair of sweatpants off the floor and tug them on. Yanking the door open, she stomps into the living area and I rush out after her. She's glaring at Faye, and Faye stares at me in confusion. "Call me some time," she says to Ky, roaming his body with hungry eyes. "I have a feeling you'll be in need of new female company soon." Casting another glare at Faye, she storms out of the apartment leaving a mess in her wake.

"What the hell is that chick's problem?" Faye asks Ky, her fists clenched into balls of fury at her side. "What a bitch! She hit on you right in front of me." A red flush creeps up her neck, and her eyes blaze with unconcealed anger.

"Babe." Ky draws her into his arms. "Ignore her. She's obviously sore because you interrupted, and clearly, she didn't get her rocks off." He levels an amused look my way.

"Neither of us did," I growl. "Thanks for that by the way." The amused expression drops off Ky's face, and his uber-protective mode cranks up a notch. He's getting ready to chew me out. Not that he needs to. Faye is more than capable of standing her ground, but Ky loves to go all alpha-protector. "Sorry," I add quickly, before he can lay into me. "It's not your fault I lost track of time."

"I was going to say I'm sorry for ruining your fun, but after the way that bitch acted, I think I've just done you a massive favor, Brad," Faye proclaims.

Well, fuck me. Can my warped life get any more warped?

♥♥♥♥♥♥

"Why did Rachel go back to Ireland anyway?" I ask from the backseat of Ky's Range Rover en route to Logan Airport.

"She had to pack up the rest of her stuff, and her parents wanted to talk to her about something," Faye confirms, shifting around in the passenger seat so she's facing me.

"And she's really moving here for good?" I look absently out the window as Ky takes the exit for the airport.

"Yep." Faye can't contain her excitement. "It's going to be so cool having her here. And the apartment she bought for us to share is incredible. It's in a fabulous building only minutes' walk from Harvard. She got the best unit on the top floor, and we have our own rooms with walk-in wardrobes and en suite bathrooms and our own outside decked area. And they have this amazing communal rooftop deck too, parking, Wi-Fi, twenty-four-hour concierge, and even a gym," she gushes, sighing dreamily. "It sure beats living in the freshman dorms."

"Breathe, babe." Ky pins her with an amused look. "And you *wanted* to live in the dorms last year."

She twists around in her seat, the leather making a squelching sound in the process. "I know, and I'm glad I experienced it, but I'm happy to be moving out and moving in with someone I know and trust."

Ky squeezes her thigh. "Me too, and I'm glad you're away from Becca. That girl gave me the creeps."

Faye's roomie last year took more than a little liking to Ky. It didn't seem to matter that he was besotted with his girlfriend—she pestered him all of fall semester to the point of harassment. Ky threatened to report her and organized a transfer for Faye to a single dorm, and, thankfully, that was the end of her interference. But it added a lot of unnecessary drama to our freshman year.

Faye shudders. "I know. That girl was genuinely scary."

"It's behind us now." Ky looks at her so adoringly—in what is his usual way—and a pang of envy has a vise-grip on my heart. It's so difficult to be around them, and that whole situation with Becca meant Faye spent an inordinate amount of time in our apartment those first few months, which only added to my torture. I enjoyed a lot of hookups and one-night stands in the early Harvard days. Anything to not have to return home and listen to my friend banging the hell out of the girl I love.

While Faye and Ky returned to Wellesley for summer break, I chose to stay in our apartment, needing the headspace. One of the guys from the football team moved in with me, and we spent the summer partying up a storm, only toning things down the last few weeks once early practice sessions started up. Coach takes a dim view of excessive partying, and I've been privy to more than a few lectures over the course of the last year. Still, it's hard for him to find fault when I'm keeping good grades and playing well.

Faye stretches over the console to kiss Ky, and bile swims up my throat.

Closing my eyes, I rest my head against the window, praying to God to release me from this hell.

"I've a good feeling about this year. Our sophomore year is going to be great. For all of us," Faye says softly. My eyes fly open, just catching the hopeful look she sends my way. I pray she's right, because the prospect of spending another year locked in this awkward love triangle doesn't bear thinking about. I don't think I'll survive another year of the same. There is only so much a guy can take before he cracks.

Faye returns Ky's adoring gaze, reaching across to tenderly caress his face.

My heart aches again, and I slump a little in my seat, awash with a whole array of conflicted emotions. Sometimes, I wish I could just remove my brain and all the accompanying futile thoughts and enjoy the nothingness. The complete and utter silence that would be a welcome relief.

Rachel's flight has already landed by the time we park, and we race through the airport to reach arrivals before she walks out.

About two minutes after we arrive, she emerges through the gate looking even more beautiful than I remember. Her gorgeous dark hair is loose and flowing in thick waves down her back. She is wearing fitted skinny jeans that hug her curves in all the right places and a flimsy white blouse over a snug white lacy tank top. Moving confidently in her strappy stilettos, she removes her large sunglasses, propping them on top of her head as she notices Faye running toward her. The girls hug as Ky takes ahold of Rachel's suitcase, returning to my side.

"You doing okay?" He glances sideways at me.

"I'm fine," I say, more harshly than necessary.

He levels a serious look at me. "What was up with the girl earlier?"

I shrug. "Who knows? We weren't doing much talking."

He scrubs a hand over his cheek. "I know things are rough, man, but screwing your way through campus again this year isn't the answer. And it's not who you are."

"I don't give you advice on your love life, so don't try to inject yourself into mine," I hiss. "I'm sick of everyone trying to tell me what to do. It's my life, and I'll live it the way I want to."

He sighs, and I watch as the girls loop arms, heading in our direction. "That's bullshit, man, and you know it. Fine if you don't want to confide in me. I get it. But at least confide in *someone*."

What's the frigging point? Talking about it isn't going to solve the issue. I have no clue how to fix this clusterfuck I find myself in. I should never have suggested I act as Faye's fake boyfriend during senior year of high school. That's really when all the problems started. I was already attracted to her looks and her personality, so putting myself in that position was a recipe for disaster. But I thought I was helping Ky out. His troublesome ex was blackmailing him, and he was concerned she would target Faye if she knew he was falling for her. So, we agreed the best form of protection was to pretend I was her boyfriend, to hide her true relationship.

By the time our fake relationship was over, I was already head over heels in love with her. I should never have allowed my heart to become invested, but it was difficult to remain detached when we spent so much time together. We were going through similar things at the time, and we connected in a way I've never connected with any girl before. She became a good friend. And so much more. While Faye had a strict no-kissing policy in place, we held hands and were openly affectionate for months. She stole my heart before I even realized it.

And let's not forget the two times we had kissed before she cemented her relationship with my best friend. I can still remember how soft her lips were. How good it felt to hold her in my arms.

Reliving those memories is killing me, but I must love torturing myself, because I can't stop thinking about her. She's the only girl I want even though I know she will never be mine.

And I hate that there's constant tension in my relationship with Ky. We've known each other since we were two, and this is driving a wedge between us. Ky and I used to be able to talk to each other about anything, and I miss it. He's the brother I always wished I had—not to disparage my two sisters whom I miss so Goddamned much—but, growing up, Ky was my de facto brother, and I never thought the time would come when a girl came between us.

And it's not like this is an isolated case.

Addison was the first girl to drive a stake through the heart of our friendship, and our relationship never had time to recover from that fuck-up before this new one kicked off.

The girls land in front of us. "Look who came with," Faye says to Rachel, wiggling her eyebrows as she stares at me.

I jerk my chin up, shoving my hands in my pockets. "Red."

Her lips purse before speaking. "Dickhead."

And I am a dickhead. I know she doesn't like to be called that, and it's not exactly fitting any more considering her hair is no longer the garish red it was when we first met, but I know it pisses her off, and I want her to stay mad at me. Rachel has some stupid notion in her head that we can be friends, and I'm determined to quash that idea before it takes root.

Friendship with a girl as hot as Rachel would only lead to sex, and I don't go back for seconds.

*** END OF SAMPLE ***

AVAILABLE NOW

INSEPARABLE

A gritty, angsty, friends-to-lovers standalone romance.

A childhood promise. An unbreakable bond. One tragic event that shatters everything.

It all started with the boys next door...

Devin and Ayden were my best friends. We were practically joined at the hip since age two. When we were kids, we thought we were invincible, inseparable, that nothing or no one could come between us.

But we were wrong.

Everything turned to crap our senior year of high school.

Devin was turning into a clone of his deadbeat lowlife father—fighting, getting wasted, and screwing his way through every girl in town. I'd been hiding a secret crush on him for years. Afraid to tell him how I felt in case I ruined everything. So, I kept quiet and slowly watched him self-destruct with a constant ache in my heart.

Where Devin was all brooding darkness, Ayden was the shining light. Our star quarterback with the bright future whom everyone loved. But something wasn't right. He was so guarded, and he wouldn't let me in.

When Devin publicly shamed me, Ayden took my side, and our awesome-threesome bond was severed. The split was devastating. The heartbreak inevitable.

Ayden and I moved on with our lives, but the pain never lessened, and Devin was never far from our thoughts.

Until it all came to a head in college, and one eventful night changed everything.

Now, I've lost the two people who matter more to me than life itself. Nothing will ever be the same again.

AVAILABLE NOW

INSEPARABLE-SAMPLE PROLOGUE

Present Day – Angelina

Life is just a flow of interconnecting moments in time. A combination of well-thought-out actions and spontaneous reactions. A sequence of events and people moving in and out of your personal stratosphere.

At least, that's how I've always viewed it.

Like a squiggly line veering up and down with no apparent pattern. Plotting the highs; pinpointing the lows. Showcasing the happy times. Highlighting the mistakes and the resulting consequences. Calling into focus all the myriad of things I should've done differently if I had known.

When I was a kid, I was obsessed with the notion of time—making a beeline for the fortune teller every year when the carnival descended on the wide, open grassy field just outside town. I saved my pocket money all year round so I could have my fortune told. The idea that you could see into the future, to know what was around the corner, held an enormous fascination for me.

I wanted to make something of my life.

To dedicate myself to a profession that helped others.

To know happiness awaited me.

To receive confirmation that the two most important people in my life would always be in it. Because even the thought I could lose Ayden or Devin always sent horrific tremors of fear rushing through me.

For as long as I can remember, it had always been the three of us. Best friends to the end. The awesome-threesome. Forever infinity. It was a friendship more akin to family. A meeting of minds and hearts and promises. A connection so deep that we swore nothing or no one would ever come between us. We committed ourselves in a secret bond when we were twelve, and the commitment was imprinted on my heart in the same way it was inked on my skin.

I could never have predicted what was to come.

That I'd be the one to destroy everything.

No fortune teller *ever* told me that.

For years, I've thought of nothing but the what-ifs and obsessed over so many questions.

What if a fortune teller had told me what would come to pass?

Would things have been different?

What would I change?

Would I have had the strength to stay away from my two best friends? To forge a completely different path in life? To deny something that was intrinsically a part of myself? Could I slice my heart apart knowing it was the right thing to do?

For years these questions have plagued me.

But I'm too afraid to confront the truth, even though it's front and center. Even though I carry it with me like a thundercloud, hovering and threatening but never opening up, never letting the storm loose.

Some truths are far too painful to acknowledge out loud.

As if to speak the words would confirm what I already know about myself.

That I'm weak, selfish, and not at all the person I thought I was.

Perhaps that's why we don't have that cognitive ability—to see the future, to know what lies ahead. I've thought of it often. If it's evolution. If at some time in the future humans will be able to sense the path of their destiny. To alter their fate. To assume full control over every aspect of their life with conscious decision.

For now, all I've got is that squiggly line and a huge helping of regret.

What good comes from continually looking back? From locking myself in the haunted mansion of my past? Meandering with the ghosts of guilt and shame? For a girl who spent her happy youth so focused on the future, it's a very sorry state of affairs. But I'm stuck in this washing machine that is my so-called life. The faster it churns, the more I lose myself. So, I try to stop time. To stand still. To numb myself to my reality. To blank out feeling and emotion. To close myself off. To never allow another human to imprint on my heart or to see into the black, murky depths of my soul.

The honest truth is, if I'd had a crystal ball—if I'd known what was going to happen—I still wouldn't have changed a thing.

Because I would've missed those high points. Those happy memories that are the only thing keeping me alive right now.

If that's what you can call my current existence.

And that makes me the most selfish, conceited liar on the planet.

PART I

Senior Year of High School

CHAPTER ONE
Angelina

Tap. Tap. Tap.

I emit a high-pitched shriek, almost jumping out of my skin. Blood rushes to my head as I spin around in my bedroom. Devin has his face pressed into the glass of the French doors, peering in. His nose is all smushed up, and he's wearing his trademark shit-eating grin. Dropping my book bag on the floor beside my bed, I walk over, flinging the doors open with gusto. "Dev, what the hell? Are you trying to give me a coronary?"

He saunters into my room, flopping down on the bed like he owns it, his customary grin still planted firmly on his lips. "Hey, baby doll. Come sit." He pats the bed, stretching out his long, sculpted torso before propping up on his side.

I perch on the edge of the mattress, slapping his leg. "Don't call me that. I'm not one of your conquests."

"I was thinking more along the lines of a faithful pet." He smirks, attempting to smother his laughter as he watches the scowl appear on my face.

"Don't push your luck, asshole."

"Ange." He pats the bed alongside him again. "Come here." He looks at me through hooded lashes, and his green eyes smolder in that intense way of his. Strands of his black hair fall over his forehead as his gaze bores a hole deep inside me.

Devin defines drop-dead gorgeous. With his sinful good looks, ripped body, and dark brooding intensity, it's no wonder every girl in town hangs off his every word.

Lost under the magnetism of his penetrating focus, I forget how to breathe. "Come. Here," he mouths this time, failing to hide his knowing smirk.

Yeah. Dev's well aware of the effect he has on the female population, myself included.

I sigh but give up fighting the inevitable. Toeing off my shoes, I crawl up the bed, dropping down beside him. He reaches out, twirling strands of my long, dark hair around his finger. His eyes hold mine as his fingers weave in and out of my hair, and I zone out, like I've been drugged. Clamping my lips shut, I stifle the blissful moan building at the back of my throat. His hands feel *so good* in my hair. My blood pressure soars, butterflies go crazy in the pit of my stomach, and a familiar ache throbs between my legs.

I shouldn't have these feelings for Devin, but I've been harboring them for years, and I'm sure I'm going to spontaneously combust one of these days. Pent-up frustration and potent longing are my constant companions. An incessant reminder of all that is denied to me.

He's oblivious, of course.

I'm in an exclusive ten percent club—that minuscule pool of girls in senior class who have yet to sample the Devin experience.

Although I know all about it.

The girls at school can't keep their legs or their mouths shut.

I've heard all the stories these last couple of years, and I wish I could wash my ears out and scrub my brain free of the heartbreaking knowledge. Devin is gaining quite the rep around town. And not just for his man-whore ways.

"What are you doing home on a Saturday night anyway?" I ask, while he continues threading his fingers through my hair. I'm pleased that I manage to sound semi-coherent, and it's good to know he hasn't nuked all my brain cells.

Devin is hardly ever at home anymore. Especially not on a weekend night. There are copious parties to attend and numerous willing girls to fuck. Getting laid and drunk appears to take precedence over our friendship these days, and I've had to sit back and watch it happen with a heavy heart. Most times, I only see him at school, and then it's sporadic and fleeting. Occasionally, he'll drop into the diner where I work, but those visits are becoming few and far between. It's the been the same these past few months, ever since we started our final year, and it hurts. Way more than I've let on to anyone.

I miss my best friend, and I hate that a rift has formed in our seemingly unbreakable bond. Worse is I don't understand how this has happened or why.

My other best friend and neighbor, Ayden, has been more vocal and less concerned about rocking the boat. His impatience with Devin is growing by the day, and the cracks are splintering in our friendship. I never thought I'd see the day when we were anything but joined at the hip.

Things are changing, and I don't like it.

"I wanted to see you more than I wanted to go out," he admits, startling me with his honesty.

The romantic, nostalgic, girly-girl part of my brain is ready to throw a party, but the more logical, guarded side of my brain kicks in, cautioning me to chill the fuck out. I narrow my eyes as I scrutinize his face. "Are you high or drunk right now?"

He frowns, and his hand stalls in my hair. "Of course not."

I snort. "You say that like it's outside the realm of possibility you'd be either of those things."

He removes his hand from my hair, and I feel bereft. "We both know who I am, Ange, but I'm surprised you think I'd turn up here like that. Not with you. Never with you."

"Is that supposed to make me feel special?" I blurt.

"You *are* special, and you know it." He leans in, kissing the top of my head, and his chest brushes against mine, sending a flurry of fiery tingles whipping through me. Heat from his body washes over me, and I close my eyes, praying for self-control. The urge to touch him is almost overpowering. It's one of the reasons why I haven't pushed him as much as Ayden. If we were to start spending more time together, I don't know that I could contain my feelings. As it is, I don't know how much longer I can continue to hide them.

I've spent years crushing on Devin, and I'm close to my breaking point.

A sharp, stabbing pain pierces me straight through the heart.

I shouldn't feel this way about one of my best friends, but I can't help it. I've been in love with him for so long, even if he doesn't have a clue.

He doesn't look at me like that.

Neither of my besties do, and that's the way it should be.

I'm the one stuck with faulty internal wiring. We have grown up as close as three kids can be. He should be like a brother to me. In a lot of ways, he is.

But, God, he's so much more.

"How'd you get on my balcony anyway?" I ask, the thought suddenly occurring to me.

He drops his head onto my pillow, chuckling. "How do you think?"

My mouth falls open, and I slap him across the chest. "Devin Robert Morgan, you did *not* climb the tree?!" He sends me a devilish wink, and I slap his chest again. "You idiot! You're not a kid anymore, and you're lucky you made it in one piece." Devin is well over six-foot tall and while he doesn't have Ayden's football player's body, he has a toned, muscular physique that has all the girls drooling.

Yours truly included.

"Chill. Old Man Willow can handle my awesomeness."

My bedroom is at the back of our house, and I have my own private balcony. An old oak tree holds court directly outside my room, its spindly branches like giant fingers stretching toward our house. When we were younger, the boys used to climb the tree in the dead of night and jump over onto my balcony. Mom never knew, and thus began a weekly tradition that spanned years.

Every Friday night, Devin and Ayden climbed that tree to my room. And every Friday night, we sat up until the early hours, whispering, laughing, and watching the stars. We went through a *Lord of the Rings* phase one year, and Devin likened the tree in my yard to the willow tree in Tolkien's legendary tale, and, henceforth it became known by the same name.

Our Friday night tradition ceased when the boys stretched up and out and became too big to climb it. It also coincided with the time of Devin's transformation—when he morphed into one of the town's most notorious bad boys.

"You know my mom works the night shift in the hospital almost every Saturday night. You could've just used the front door."

"And where's the fun in that?" he quips, smirking, and I roll my eyes. "Wanna hang out on the balcony? For old time's sake?"

I examine his face, noting a vulnerability I haven't seen in a long time. My chest tightens in awareness. Something brought him here tonight. Something forced him to seek out my company.

Not that I'm in any way complaining. The last thing I'd ever do is deny him anything. Even if his actions unconsciously continue to hurt me. "Sure. That'd be fun. I'll get some snacks. Can you grab a couple blankets from my closet?"

"You're the boss."

I arch a brow, and he chuckles. "Glad you know the lay of the land." I grin, before throwing caution to the wind. "We should call Ayden." I know he's visiting his grandma in the nursing home—he always goes with his mom the last Saturday of every month—but he'll be back soon.

"No." Devin's reply is swift and laced with determination.

"Don't tell me you two aren't speaking again?" It's a familiar pattern these last few months, since something went down between them during summer break, and I hate it. Hate all the tension and discord. All the fighting.

"That's not it. I just…" He trails off, looking down at his feet. "I just want to be alone with you." He lifts his head, and I'm surprised to see such raw, naked emotion glistening in his eyes. I feel his pain as acutely as if it's my own. It's like I've been punched in the gut. "I need you, Ange," he whispers.

I step toward him without thinking, planting my hand on his rock-hard chest. His heart beats steadily under my palm through the thin material of his shirt. "I'm always here for you. Always. You never have to doubt that."

He cups my face, peering deep into my eyes. "You're way too good to me. You should hate me."

My brow furrows. "Why on earth would I hate you?" Devin is trampling all over my heart, but he doesn't know that, and it's not like he's doing it on purpose. He can screw whomever he likes, and it's none of my business. Doesn't matter that every girl, every kiss and every caress I'm witness to, adds another scar to my heart. Outwardly, there is no reason why he should feel like this, so I don't understand what's going on in his head.

"Because this ... this divide between us is all my fault."

I skim my hand up his arm, and he flinches slightly. Heat seeps from his skin through my fingertips, igniting my blood and fueling my desire. I gulp, trying to put a leash on my lust. "It's all our faults, and it's not too late to fix it." I peer into his eyes and start drowning. We stare at one another, and an electrical current charges the air. My chest heaves up and down, and his gaze flits to my mouth. His heart thuds more powerfully under my touch. Butterflies swarm my gut as I grapple with the situation. His eyes darken, and his pupils dilate as he continues to stare at my mouth. I don't know what's going on, but the tides are changing. Fate is swirling—I sense it, feel it, as if it's corporeal.

Is this just me or is he feeling something too?

He jerks back suddenly, and the connection is broken. Heat floods my cheeks, and I shake my head of all errant thoughts. Thinking such thoughts will only earn me a world of trouble, and I could do without that this year. "I'll get the snacks," I mumble, exiting the room as quickly as my feet will carry me.

*** END OF SAMPLE ***

AVAILABLE NOW

About The Author

USA Today bestselling author **Siobhan Davis** writes emotionally intense young adult and new adult fiction with swoon-worthy romance, complex characters, and tons of unexpected plot twists and turns that will have you flipping the pages beyond bedtime! She is the author of the international bestselling *True Calling*, *Saven*, and *Kennedy Boys* series.

Siobhan's family will tell you she's a little bit obsessive when it comes to reading and writing, and they aren't wrong. She can rarely be found without her trusty Kindle, a paperback book, or her laptop somewhere close at hand.

Prior to becoming a full-time writer, Siobhan forged a successful corporate career in human resource management.

She resides in the Garden County of Ireland with her husband and two sons.

You can connect with Siobhan in the following ways:

Author Website: www.siobhandavis.com
Author Blog: My YA NA Book Obsession
Facebook: AuthorSiobhanDavis
Twitter: @siobhandavis
Google+: SiobhanDavisAuthor
Email: siobhan@siobhandavis.com

Glossary Of Irish Words And Phrases

The explanation listed is taken in the context of this book.
Bloody » Damn
Blow in » Newcomer
Cop it » Get it/Figure it out
Dart » Train
Fecked » Fucked
Fit » Hot
Footpath » Sidewalk
GAA » Irish sporting institution. (They oversee Irish Soccer and Irish Hurling tournaments which are played seasonally during the year)
Garda Station » Police Station
Gents » Male Bathroom
Gob » Mouth
Grand » Fine/Okay
Halo » Uber/Taxi
Jelly » Jell-O
Knickers » Panties
Mum » Mom
Right State » Mess
Sort/Sorted » Fix/Fixed
Wardrobe » Closet

Books By Siobhan Davis

TRUE CALLING SERIES
Young Adult Science Fiction/Dystopian Romance

True Calling
Lovestruck
Beyond Reach
Light of a Thousand Stars
Destiny Rising
Short Story Collection
True Calling Series Collection

SAVEN SERIES
Young Adult Science Fiction/Paranormal Romance

Saven Deception
The Logan Collection
Saven Disclosure
Saven Denial
Saven Defiance
The Heir and the Human
Saven Deliverance
Saven: The Complete Series

KENNEDY BOYS SERIES
Upper Young Adult/New Adult Contemporary Romance

Finding Kyler
Losing Kyler
Keeping Kyler

The Irish Getaway
Loving Kalvin
Saving Brad
Seducing Kaden
*Forgiving Keven^*
*Adoring Keaton^*
*Releasing Keanu^*
*Reforming Kent^*

STANDALONES
New Adult Contemporary Romance

Inseparable
Incognito
*When Forever Changes**

Reverse Harem Contemporary Romance

*Surviving Amber Springs**

ALINTHIA SERIES
Upper YA/NA Paranormal Romance/Reverse Harem

The Lost Savior
The Secret Heir
The Warrior Princess
*The Chosen One^*

* Coming 2018
^ Release date to be confirmed.

Visit www.siobhandavis.com for all future release dates. Release dates are subject to change based on reader demand and the author's schedule. Subscribing to the author's newsletter or following her on Facebook is the best way to stay updated with planned new releases.